Magenta

Other  titles

Magenta goes Green

ECHO FREER

Hodder
Children's
Books

a division of Hachette Children's Books

Acknowledgements: I would like to thank the following people for their support: my husband Frank for his inspirational brainstorming sessions; my children, Imogen, Verien and Jacob for their contributions and advice; Magic Mo for her proofreading ability; Adam Evans for his outward-boundiness (if there isn't such a word there ought to be); Dr Seema Gulati and Dr Michael Kelly for lending me their names (if not in this book, then in previous Magenta books) and my agent Caroline Montgomery and editor Rachel Wade, for all their hard work. Not forgetting, of course, my late brother Martin Freer Sunley – for being who he was! God bless him.

First published in Great Britain in 2006
by Hodder Children's Books

This edition published in 2007

A Catalogue record for this book is available from
the British Library

ISBN-13: 978 0 340 95075 3

Typeset in Baskerville by Avon DataSet Ltd, Bidford-on-Avon, Warks

Printed in the UK by CPI Bookmarque, Croydon, CR0 4TD

The paper and board used in this paperback by Hodder Children's
Books are natural recyclable products made from wood grown in
sustainable forests. The manufacturing processes conform to the
environmental regulations of the country of origin.

Hodder Children's Books
a division of Hachette Children's Books
338 Euston Road
London NW1 3BH

For Frarnie, with all my love.

1
Magenta

Honestly! Boys! I will never understand them. Take Daniel. For anyone who's not up to scratch on my life, I've known Daniel for ten years and for the first nine and a half of those, it was brilliant. He was my best boy mate and we'd talk about stuff and he'd make me laugh. My mum died when I was three and after that my dad and I moved in with my gran, Florence, next door to Daniel's family. I've got this really cool bedroom at the front of the house that's got French windows out on to a balcony. It was brilliant when Daniel and I were friends because we had bedrooms next to each other with adjoining balconies – so we'd be in and out of each other's rooms all the time. He really was the next best thing to a girl mate. But then I contracted temporary insanity and ended up going out with him – which was so not the way to go!

So, when I say, 'Take Daniel,' I mean it; take him anywhere – preferably somewhere far away and very cold – like Siberia.

I mean, can you believe it? Daniel has only gone

and dumped me! Dumped *me*! And after everything I put up with last term from him – his older woman and his two-timing and his drooling over my cousin. And all because I made one teensy little error of judgement (which, to be honest, wasn't even an error of judgement – I'm only saying that because Belinda, my dad's fiancée, said each person in the relationship should make some concessions and try to meet halfway). It was a total misunderstanding – and not on my part either. Although, sticking with the 'error of judgement' theme, if I did make an error of judgement it was when I agreed to go out with Daniel in the first place.

OK, so I know our relationship has had more ups and downs than your average rollercoaster but I thought things were going fairly well after the whole saving-my-life incident last term when the school play went up in smoke. He was so brave when he leaped on to the stage and rescued me and he hardly complained at all when he ended up with a broken leg. And he was *so* gorgeous the way he limped about on his crutches – really cute (in a Long John Silvery sort of way). I even (stupidly) thought that this could be the romance of the decade – yeah right! Deluded or what?

But then this 'Love at First Sight' thing kicked off.

And that isn't referring to me and Daniel either (as if!). It was this fund-raising event at school where three boys and three girls from different tutor groups have to ask each other questions and then choose the most suitable person to go on a pretend date with. I mean, how cheap is that? They weren't even going to pay for anyone to actually go out; it was all supposed to be a bit of fun and end with a kiss. And the rest of the year group were expected to fork out to watch! (Which just shows you how sad our school is.)

Now I know, strictly speaking, I wasn't actually free to go in for it because I was going out with Daniel at the time (which, by the way, is his *entire* argument for the prosecution) but in my defence:

1) No one else in our form was up for it – apart from Chelsea Riordan, who'd just split with her ex after six months and was doing the rebound thing like a yoyo on a bungee jump, and Janet Dibner, the form dork whose fashion sense comes from a 1950s knitting pattern and who is so desperate for a boyfriend she'll snog anything on two legs.

2) It was for charity and if having to give some geeky boy a teensy little peck on the cheek could help to raise money for the local old folks' home, then who am I to deny them that? Mrs

Delaney (alias Mrs Blobby, my head of year) is always droning on about giving something back to the community, so I looked on this as my contribution to society.

3) Even though I had a sneaky suspicion that Daniel might not totally approve, I didn't think he'd find out about it because he was still on crutches and The Crusher (Mr Crusham, our revered Head – not!) had refused to allow him into school on the grounds of health and safety. And I hoped that if Daniel did find out he'd understand what a wonderful thing I was doing for our school, the wrinklies in Park Lodge and the world in general.

4) Like I said, it was only pretend.

And – most importantly,

5) Billy O'Dowd, who's on parole from the behavioural unit, tricked me!

Ms Bignell, our teensy little stick insect of a PE teacher, was supposed to be arranging the Year 9 event for Charity Week and she was having major hassle getting people to show even the remotest interest – from our tutor group anyway.

'Come on now – please. You only need one more girl volunteer.' We all feel sorry for Ms Bignell – ever since last year's Year 11s locked her in the PE cupboard and she wasn't found until the caretaker did his rounds at about five o'clock – but not sorry enough to volunteer for her lame idea to raise money.

It was registration and Mr Kingston, our form tutor, was standing at the front next to Big Nell trying to look all stern and sergeant-majory, and, to give him his due, he made a pretty good job of going from his usual extreme left-wing politics to the far right in one single sentence.

'OK, I know we live in a democratic society where there's free choice in most things except death and taxes but a lot of people have made a great deal of effort to raise money for Park Lodge so, if one more girl doesn't volunteer within the next sixty seconds, the whole form will be in detention for a week.'

Like, hello! Emotional blackmail, or what? There was this universal groan and then Billy O'Dowd whispered from the table behind me, 'Hey, look out, Magenta – you've got a tarantula crawling up your arm.'

Now, call me gullible but no way was I going to sit back and assume that he was winding me up.

'Eeek!' I shrieked, lifting up my arm to check.

'Well done, Magenta. That's very noble of you,' Big Nell said, writing my name on her clipboard.

'No!' I tried to protest but I was too late.

'Let's have a round of applause for Magenta, who's just saved you lot from a week of detentions,' Mr Kingston chipped in.

So you see, the teachers recognised that what I was doing was noble and the rest of my tutor group were pretty grateful too – it was just the timing that was unfortunate.

I knew that Daniel had had an appointment at the hospital the morning of the game show but what I didn't know was that he'd had a plastic heel fitted to his plaster so that he could put weight on it. The Crusher had said he could come back to school – which was brilliant in terms of me not having to carry all his school work home every day (I was dangerously close to developing biceps like Arnold Schwarzenegger – which is so not good on a girl) but, in terms of my relationship, it couldn't have been worse.

There we were: me, Chelsea and Janet, sitting on stools on the stage in full view of the entire year group when Big Nell wheeled in the boys and, just my luck, they were the ones from Daniel's posse: Angus Lyle (the twisted fire-starter who takes pyromania to new heights) and Sam Pudmore (aka Spud, the phantom snogger whose brace got locked on to mine at the youth club disco last year and resulted in five hours in A & E and some severe lip lacerations). Oh joy! Not only were they both Daniel's mates, but they were also about as fanciable as a pair of toads with halitosis. Although, I have to say, Spud's had his rail-track brace replaced with a retainer so he looks marginally less like Rubber-band Man. Anyway, just when I was beginning to think they'd scraped the barrel for the school's most unattractive males and that the pensioners in Park Lodge would need to show some pretty hefty appreciation for what I was about to go through, on walked the third contestant.

Oh! My! God! Chelsea Riordan and I looked at each other and nearly fell off our stools. It was the new boy, Chad Albright, whose dad's a doctor and is over here from America on a year's exchange. And he is sooooo gorgeous!

I looked out into the crowd to where the rest of our tutor group were sitting. Seema and Arlette were jiggling about in their seats and giving me the thumbs-up. Ms Bignell stepped forward.

'All right, Janet, ask your question to the boys.'

Janet Dibner went the colour of an overripe tomato and began to giggle. 'I help my parents to run their boarding kennels. What's your favourite type of dog and why? To number—'

But before she could finish, Angus Lyle almost fell off his stool to answer. 'A hot dog – preferably barbecued!' Then he flicked his hand so that his fingers snapped together and began rocking like a maniac. I think there are serious sanity questions to be raised in the Lyle household – although his twin brother, Magnus, seems to have escaped the idiot gene.

Anyway, Spud gave some pretty boring answer, like, 'A spaniel because they're loyal and cute, like me.' Yuk, yuk, yuk! And what he actually meant was, 'Because they've got floppy ears and scraggly hair, like me!'

But then Chad Albright answered in this gorgeous American accent that made me feel like a herd of butterflies was looping the loop in my tummy. 'Probably a red setter because they're sleek and elegant and I love anything with red in its name.' And then, I swear, he smiled this really dreamy smile right at me! I could hardly believe it.

Each boy and each girl had to ask a question and when it got to my turn I felt really nervous. Arlette and Seema had helped me prepare my question and, I must admit, at first I thought it was a bit dorky but, in view of Chad Albright's answer to Janet Dibner, it was brilliant.

'My name's Magenta, which is a deep purplish red colour. If you could be called a colour, what colour would you choose and why?' I looked Chad right in the eye and said, 'To number three, please.'

Chad stepped down from his stool and faced the audience. 'Like I said, I like anything with red in its name because red is hot and passionate.' And he winked at me – wow! I was finding it pretty hard to remember that I had a boyfriend, I can tell you. 'And,' he went on, 'everyone knows that red and blue make purple, so if I had to be a colour, I'd choose a cool ice blue then the two of us could mix it up a bit and make everyone else green with envy.'

Ohmigod! I thought my jaw was going to hit the floor. I mean, I know it was a game about flirting, but honestly! How full on was that? I was so glad Daniel wasn't there.

And then, when everyone had asked their questions, the boys had to choose one of us to go on an imaginary date with and, this is the tricky part – both Spud *and* Chad Albright picked me! I must admit, I was a teensy bit flattered. Angus Lyle chose Chelsea but poor Janet Dibner didn't get picked – it was like a rounders lesson all over again. So, anyway, there was no way I was going to go on a date with Spud after the hideous brace-al lockage incident last term, so I agreed to go with Chad and let Janet have Spud. I mean, it was only a bit of fun and it *was* for charity, so there was no harm done, was there? Until Chad strutted across the stage, flung me backwards over his arm like they do in old films and kissed me – on the lips – in public!

The whole hall erupted with cheers and wolf whistles. I was sooooo embarrassed! I mean, don't get me wrong, Chad is tall and gorgeous with a smile like a toothpaste advert and any other time I'd have been seriously tempted – but I had a boyfriend!

Anyway, I went and sat back down with Seema and Arlette to watch the other groups go through their routines.

'Two boys chose me,' I whispered to Arlette. 'How popular am I?'

Arlette gave me a sideways glance and said, 'Not very if you'd seen Daniel's face.'

'Daniel?' I was shocked. 'He's not in school.'

Arlette shrugged. 'Well that must've been an apparition that walked in with his leg in plaster and sat next to Magnus Lyle.'

After I'd been conned into taking part in this fund-raising activity, I'd bribed Daniel's friends to keep quiet by promising them various food items (although Angus had requested a box of matches instead). Arlette had been a bit snotty about it at first.

'I think you'll find that's what's known as corruption,' she'd said. Honestly, she can be so self-righteous sometimes!

'Corruption? What is so corrupt about trying to protect Daniel's feelings?'

'Darrr! It's deceitful.'

I was beginning to think that Arlette had secretly taken holy orders or something; after all, her family are pillars of the God Squad. But then I remembered that she'd had a thing for Daniel for ages and before Christmas they'd even gone out together for a while – which put a totally new complexion on the situation.

'So, d'you want to borrow my new top this weekend?' I'd sneakily asked her.

'What, the one with all the layers? Cool!'

You see, everyone has their price and at the end of the day, it was all in a good cause and the only person who was worse off was me.

So I really thought I'd covered every angle. What I hadn't bargained for was Daniel being there in person. And I have to say, I'm pretty sure I detected a certain smugness in Arlette's voice when she told me.

'Where?' I turned round to look for him but he

wasn't there. Spud and Angus had left the stage and were sitting with Magnus and there was a spare seat at the end of their row, but no sign of Daniel. Phew! Arlette'd obviously been winding me up. 'Oh, ha ha, Arl. Very funny,' I snapped.

'Well he's not there now,' she said. 'He looked really upset from the minute you walked on stage but when you let Chad bend you backwards and kiss you like that, he just got up and limped out. I was going to go after him but Seema stopped me.'

I couldn't believe what I was hearing. 'Er, hello! I *let* Chad bend me backwards and kiss me?'

'I know – the whole year saw it.'

'I did not *let* him – he just did it!'

'Try telling that to poor Daniel,' she said, folding her arms and looking the other way.

Gggrrr! I leaned across her and whispered to Seema, 'Was Daniel really here?' I was trying very hard to keep my voice down but people were starting to turn round and shush me.

Seema nodded and I'm sure I detected a hint of 'I told you so' in there. Honestly, I really need to re-evaluate my circle of friends. But just then a voice like a rampaging bull boomed along the aisle. It was the great pink blob herself.

'Magenta Orange! My room – NOW!'

Brilliant! That was all I needed. I spend so much time in the office of my head of year that I'm thinking of applying for citizenship. As soon as the door was shut, she started.

'Other people had the decency to be quiet while you were on the stage . . . blah blah blah . . . show *them* some courtesy . . . blah blah blah . . . rude . . . blah blah . . . selfish . . .' And she rambled on and on – to be honest, I switched off. I was desperately thinking of how I could find Daniel and explain everything to him when words filtered through that set alarm bells ringing: '. . . have to think whether or not to rescind the offer to go to summer camp.'

Aha! Got her!

'I wasn't chosen to go to camp, Mrs Bl— Delaney,' I said in my most innocent voice – but secretly thinking that I'd got one over on her.

'No, not originally.' She looked as though she was mulling something over and I didn't like the look of it. 'But Deepa Dhami has moved, so her place has become available and your name was drawn out of a hat to replace her. Mr Kingston was going to tell you at this afternoon's dismissal and a letter was sent to your father this morning informing him.'

Whoa! Camp? No way! Let me explain something about our school. Every summer term The Crusher thinks it's a good idea to send a few unfortunate Year 9s on an outward-bound trip. He says it strengthens character and is a bonding experience for all concerned. Yeah, right! Excuse me if I'd rather be bonded to my nice comfy bed than sleeping in some stony, cow-patty field, under a sheet of very flimsy canvas, eating char-grilled baked beans and getting bitten by midges! That sounds about as much fun as poking myself in the eye with a sharp stick.

I must admit, when the list went up last September I did get a teensy bit carried away and bought into the whole excitement thing that Seema and Arlette were generating. They were all, 'Ooo, it'll be great.' And, 'Ooo, we can have so much fun.' And, 'Ooo, we can have midnight feasts.' So, in a passing phase of brain fever, I put my name down. Fortunately, I wasn't picked and, even though both my best mates were selected and I knew it would mean spending a week in school with practically only Janet Dibner and Billy O'Dowd for company, believe me, I was very relieved.

And I didn't think any more about it. But now it seemed, Fate had dealt me a very cruel blow. I had to think fast. I lowered my eyes and cocked my head on one side, like Sirius my dog does when he's eaten Dad's slippers or peed on the curtains again.

'I'm very sorry, Mrs Delaney,' I said, with just a hint of a sniffle in there, so that she'd think I was crying. 'I didn't know I'd been chosen to go to camp and it would've been so much fun but, if it's my punishment not to go, then I accept it.'

I looked up to try and assess her reaction but it didn't look too promising. Her eyes, which at the best of times are so small that they border on the piggy, were reduced to suspicious slits.

'Let me remind you, Magenta, I have been teaching for longer than I care to remember and I can smell a double bluff a mile off.' Oops! 'Perhaps a week at camp will do you good.' She was nodding in this really smug way. 'Yes, I think I'll telephone your father this evening and explain the situation.' Oh, brilliant! That's all I need – my dad on my case too. 'And, just to let you into a little secret . . .' she said in this falsely friendly way that made me want to throw, '. . .the girls' chaperones will be Ms Bignell . . .' (Which was cool because she's such a pushover that I started to think maybe camp could be fun after all.) '. . . Miss Crumm . . .' (Oh no! Rewind. She's the head of PE who has all the physical attributes of a rhinoceros, combined with the personality of a psychotic Rottweiler. I couldn't think of anyone I would less like to spend a week with.) '. . . and, of course, myself.' OK – I was wrong. There *is* someone I would less like to spend a week with.

And then, as if my life wasn't totally ruined, on my way out of The Blob's room I only went and saw Daniel (the skunk) sitting in the foyer next to Kara Kennedy – the school fitness freak – and she had her arm round his shoulder! Talk about a fast worker! I was fuming (and also a teensy bit guilty because I thought he might have got the wrong end of the stick about the whole Love at First Sight thing). So, I hid behind one of the pillars in the foyer. Honestly, I couldn't believe my eyes. The worm was all over her like the plague – anyone would think he didn't have a girlfriend. (OK, so I know my actions on the stage could have been open to slight misinterpretation – but that *was* for charity!)

And then the two of them left – together! With Kara putting her arm round his waist and everything! And that was *my* job helping Daniel around and there he was letting *her* do it.

I went straight to the girls' toilets and phoned him from my mobile. But can you believe it? It rang a couple of times and then he only went and switched it off! And this evening, he refused to come to his French window when I knocked, even though I could hear his television, so I knew he was in there.

So, reasons for me to flee the country:

1) My boyfriend is avoiding me.
2) I've got my SATs next week and, thanks to Daniel, I'm totally *not* in the mood to take exams, so if I get lousy marks like I did in the practice tests, it'll be all his fault.
3) My father has backed The Blob's decision to send me to boot camp!

Life is so unfair!

2
Daniel

Girls! I will never understand them. I thought Magenta and I were finally sorted and then this happens.

I've been crazy about her for ages, even when we were at primary school and she was into dolls and all that stuff. We did get it on before Christmas for a couple of weeks but then it all went pear-shaped. So when we got together again at the school play last term, I thought – hallelujah, this is it! It was like I'd died and gone to heaven. We'd been an item for about a month and it was brilliant. Of course, progress was hampered by the small matter of my leg being in plaster, but on the positive side, there are so many advantages to being on crutches.

a) Mum has paid for me to take cabs whenever we go out – which is a good job as my car washing business has dried up ('scuse the pun) since I've been out of action.

b) I haven't been able to do my share of the housework so my piranha-featured brother Joe has had to do double (oh yes – there is a God!).

c) Every time I've needed to go up any steps Magenta has had to put her arm round my waist to help me, which is wonderful. She's been so lovely and attentive. I think she'd make a wonderful nurse.

d) We got special seats in the cinema, right at the back and on the end of the row, which meant that we could kiss and everything without anyone gawping at us.

e) Magenta used my cast to practise her artwork and she drew this really cool picture of the two of us kissing. She's such a brilliant artist and whenever I looked at the drawing it made me go all gooey inside. I thought she was so kind and thoughtful . . . (note the past tense).

f) My arms are really toned and look as though I've been working out at the gym (although my right leg is a bit weedy but the doctor says that'll soon get back to normal once I'm walking on it again).

So, when I was told that I could have a plastic heel and put weight on my leg again, I knew I was going to miss all that, but the idea of being able to spend the daytime with Magenta was way more appealing than all the other stuff. We'd be able to walk to school together again and I'd be able to see her in the quadrangle at break and in the dining hall at lunchtime – it would be wonderful. Plus, Joe's on study leave, and he's not exactly my favourite person to have hanging around while I'm off school. Of course I was sad that they cut off the plaster with her drawing on it, but at the time I thought there was nothing to stop her doing another. In fact, I couldn't wait to get into school and show her.

After my hospital appointment, Mum dropped me off at school and I hobbled up to The Crusher's office just so that he could OK me being back on the premises. Then I headed for the hall. I knew it was Charity Week because all my mates had told me about it and I was a tad sceptical that Magenta hadn't said anything but I assumed it was because she was trying to protect me and didn't want me to think I was missing out. (Durrr! Stupid alert!)

'So what're you doing for Charity Week?' I'd asked as we were lying on my bed and she was colouring in this humungous love heart on my plaster. Oh, she was so cute the way she nibbled her bottom lip as she concentrated.

'Nothing,' she said quickly, and I have to admit, I thought she seemed a tad jumpy.

'Spud said that all Year 9s were doing this Love at First Sight thing?'

'Oh, that!' She cleared her throat and stared really hard at the drawing she was doing. 'Yeah, I think that's going ahead.'

'So who's doing it from your tutor group?' With hindsight I can see how elusive she was, but at the time I thought she was being extra attentive because she cared about my feelings.

'Erm, I'm not allowed to say,' she replied, changing the subject. 'So, are you going to be up for the Youth Centre bowling trip on Friday? My dad said he'd give us both a lift if you can manage it and, if they won't let you bowl 'cos of your plaster, we could always play pool or go on the machines or something.'

'That'd be cool,' I agreed. 'Let me guess.'

'Guess what?' she asked, putting her pens away.

'Who's going in for Love at First Sight from your form? I bet Janet Dibner was gagging to get up there.'

'Honestly, Daniel, what's the big deal? It's only some stupid game show.'

'Pity I won't be there to watch – should be fun,' I said.

'Fun? Our school would suck the fun out of anything. It'll be a load of losers making prats of themselves. Anyway, it's time I went back – I've got some homework to do.'

Now if that wasn't an alarm bell, I don't know

what was. Magenta *never* went home early to do homework. But I was so deluded with love that I wouldn't have been able to see a tidal wave on a duck pond.

Everyone was already in the hall by the time The Crusher had done his whole *Welcome back to Archimedes High* routine – anyone would think I'd been away for at least a year the way he went on. So, I slipped in just as it was starting. I could see my tutor group sitting at the back of the hall. Magnus gave me the thumbs-up and beckoned me to sit with him. As I limped down the aisle I looked round for Magenta's lot. They were ahead of ours about halfway down the hall, but I couldn't see her. Arlette was there and Seema but there was a space next to them. I thought Magenta must have been in detention or something. But then, after a couple of rounds of Love at First Sight, the group from Magenta's form went on and there she was! On the stage, taking part in a dating game!

I couldn't believe it. I went into shock. Surely it must be a mistake; maybe she was there to introduce the contestants? But then it got worse; the lads from *our* tutor group went on to chat up the girls from hers. Including Spud – the double-crossing weasel. It was like my worst nightmare. Even worse than when he'd forced a kiss on her and their braces got locked together for five hours, even worse than when she'd gone out with that monkey-brained skate-freak, Ryan Dunn.

Magnus shook his head in disbelief when he saw her. 'Oh man! That is so out of order.'

At least I had one mate I could count on. But then he sank down under the chair as Angus, his twin (who was also on stage), began rocking about like a head-banger who'd escaped from a rock concert.

'Who's that?' I whispered as this boy with shoulders like a double-decker bus and teeth that looked as though they'd been cleaned with Sparkle stepped forwards.

Magnus poked his head up and groaned. 'That, my pedigree chum, is Chad Albright; a new boy from America.'

'Chad who?'

'Albright. Albright by name and all bright by dentistry.'

And then, to my horror, the dentally gifted Chad Albright only walked across the stage, took Magenta in his arms – *my* Magenta – and kissed her! Properly! On the lips and everything! I thought I was going to chuck. It was too much. I got up and limped out of the hall.

I wanted to go home but, even though my house is just round the corner and I still had my crutches, I thought it might be stupid to try and walk on my first day back, so I went to the office and asked them to phone a cab. I told them I was in pain – which wasn't a total lie. So, while I was sitting in the foyer waiting and trying to hold on to my dignity, Kara Kennedy came up and sat next to me. Kara's OK. She's captain of the netball team and plays tennis for a local club as well as being the district two hundred metres champion.

'You OK?' she asked.

'Fine,' I managed, but I was finding it pretty hard to talk. Either my Adam's apple had suddenly swelled up to the size of a tennis ball or I was about to start blubbing – and, even without a mirror, I had the distinct impression that it wasn't the first option.

'You don't *look* fine,' she said – like she was some emotional detective or something.

'Really – I'm OK.' I didn't know why she'd come out of the hall but right at the moment I wished she'd go back in again. 'You don't need to sit with me.' It was definitely more a statement of fact than a subtle hint, but she didn't get it.

'I'm waiting for my mum to collect me; I've got an

athletics meeting tonight and it's miles away so I'm leaving early.' Just what I needed – not! And then she said the words that hit me like a pneumatic drill to the eardrums. 'You must be gutted to see your ex snogging someone else in public.'

Ex? What had been going on while I'd been away? What did Kara Kennedy know that I didn't? And why hadn't any of my so-called mates told me that I'd been dumped?

'Magenta is not my ex!' I said – fairly confidently I thought in the circumstances.

She shrugged. 'Really? Why not? No self-respecting bloke would let their girlfriend get away with that sort of behaviour.'

She was right. And I might be temporarily challenged in the leg area but I was still a self-respecting bloke, wasn't I? I suddenly went from feeling gutted to wanting to blast Magenta off the face of the Earth.

'Hey, listen,' Kara suggested, 'why don't you cancel your cab and my mum can drop you home?'

And she put her arm round my shoulder in a way that was so much more than a gesture of comfort. And, to make matters worse (or better, I haven't decided yet), when I got out of her mum's car, she leaned forwards and kissed me on the lips – just a little peck, no tongues or anything, but it was definitely on the lips.

'Do you want someone to call for you in the morning to carry your books and stuff?' she said, helping me to my door.

'Actually, I'm thinking of taking the rest of the week off.' There was no way I could face going in again.

'Cool. I can collect your work for you if you want and drop it round.'

And that's all that happened – honestly! But apparently it was enough to give the two-timing Magenta permission to go into competition with Chelsea Riordan for boy-oholic of the century because, within twenty-four hours of snogging Chad (Mr Shiny Teeth) Albright, she'd only gone and asked out Spud, my supposed mate.

It was Magnus who told me. He phoned the day after the terrible Love at First Sight episode.

'Hey, listen, mate, I don't know how to tell you this . . . but Magenta's going out with Spud.'

'What!'

'Well, to be fair,' Magnus explained, 'Kara has been shouting it all round school that you and her are an item.'

'What!' I was on my bed staring up at the poster of

Sarah Michelle Gellar on my ceiling and wishing it would crash down on top of me and bring the ceiling with it. Then they'd have to bring in sniffer dogs to search and rescue and I'd have to survive on pockets of air and dribbles of water from the tank (as long as there weren't any dead pigeons in there) and everyone would be upset and then there'd be celebrations when I was brought out alive and Magenta would hug me and it would be all right again.

'Well, are you?' Magnus snapped me back to harsh reality.

'What?' I was so shocked, I seemed to have regressed to a one-word vocabulary.

'Going out with Kara Kennedy?'

'I . . . well . . . I'm not . . .' What could I say? I didn't know whether I was or I wasn't. True, Kara had brought my school work round for me because I was still so upset with Magenta that I didn't want anything to do with her – but we could get over this, couldn't we? And just bringing someone's books round hardly constitutes a hot date, does it? 'I don't know,' I said feebly.

'Only,' Magnus went on, 'it's the bowling trip tomorrow and Angus is taking Chelsea and Spud's going with Magenta so, I thought if you *weren't* going out with Kara, I'd ask her.'

'What!' First Spud snatched the love of my life from under my nose and then my new best mate was going to take her replacement. What was this, the great girlfriend giveaway? Special offer while stocks last: get dumped by one girlfriend, lose another for free!

'Well, she is kinda hot when you see her in her tennis skirt,' Magnus said.

'No!' I said. 'No way! *I'm* going to go with Kara.'

'OK, cool it, man – I was just sounding you out.' There was a short silence and then he asked, 'You don't know if Hattie Pringle's going out with anyone do you?'

'Go for it,' I advised wearily. 'See you tomorrow.'

So I'm lying here feeling about as much like going bowling as crawling SAS-style over a field of thistles – in my boxers – in winter! But there's no way I'm going to let Spud and Magenta think they can make my life a misery. This is the new Daniel Davis talking – no more Mr Nice-guy!

3
Magenta

How amazing is that! Before you say anything, I know I said I'd never go within a ten-metre bargepole of Spud after the unmentionable brace-bonding incident, but look at it from my point of view:

a) I've been dumped for absolutely no good reason and Daniel (the rat) didn't even have the guts to tell me himself.

b) I am a free agent (as a result of the aforementioned dumping).

c) If Daniel (the mongoose) thinks I'm going to hang around mooching after him, he can think again – I am sooooo over him!

d) Spud's started tying his hair back, you know, like Indie bass players do, and I have to say, he looks quite fit – well, sometimes.

And anyway,

e) What have I got to lose?

But let me take you back to yesterday when I called for Daniel, so that I could:

1) help him to school and

2) put him straight about the Chad Albright misunderstanding.

It was so annoying because when I went across the balcony to his French window, he was still doing the whole closed curtain thing.

'Daniel – I just want to explain,' I shouted. Nothing! 'If you don't open up, you'll leave me no alternative!' I threatened. But the worm still didn't let me in. So, that was it, he'd left me no choice – I was going to have to use the front door.

'To be sure, Magenta love, Daniel found it a bit too much yesterday.' It was Mary, Daniel's mum, but at least someone had answered the door to me and I knew I hadn't accidentally donned my cloak of invisibility. 'He's going to stay home for the rest of the week, just to build up his strength.'

'Oh. OK.' I must confess, I felt a tad disappointed – but I put on a brave face. 'Does he want me to take his homework in for him?'

At that moment Joe, Daniel's brother, stumbled downstairs in his boxer shorts looking like an extra from *Night of the Waking Dead*. 'Loserrrrr!' he sneered as he shuffled past the door. Joe and I have this sort of hate/hate relationship – which suits me just fine.

'Joe!' Mary said sharply. 'There's no need for that.'

'Don't worry about him,' I reassured Mary and

then jacked it up a bit so that Joe could hear. 'He's probably just looked in a mirror!'

Joe grinned. 'Wooooo! All I can say is that at long last my little bro has had the balls to get himself a real babe.' You see – it pays to stand up for yourself. I never thought I'd see the day when Joe called me a 'real babe'.

'Joseph! Enough!' Mary snapped. 'Go and do the washing-up from last night.'

'Aw, Mum! I washed up yesterday morning.' He went off muttering, 'Daniel is so going to do double when he can stand up properly.'

Then Mary looked back at me in this weird way; sort of sad with a hint of embarrassment. 'I don't think it'll be necessary to take Daniel's books in today.'

'Or any day,' Joe shouted from the kitchen.

And then – were my eyes deceiving me? Kara Kennedy only came down the stairs carrying a whole load of Daniel's schoolbooks – at eight thirty in the morning! And she doesn't even live round here.

'Hi, Magenta,' she breezed, like it was the most natural thing in the world. 'Do you want a lift? My mum's outside in the car.'

'Durr! It only takes two minutes to walk round the corner, why would I want a lift?' I must admit, I probably sounded a teensy bit snappy but I'd rather have passed a kidney stone than two minutes in a car with Miss Biceps-of-the-Year.

'Suit yourself. Bye, Mrs Davis, I'll see you tonight.' And she flounced out.

Halfway down the path, she looked up and waved towards Daniel's window. Hmph! So, he was well enough to come to the window for *her* but he couldn't manage to stagger across to answer when I'd been knocking for him! And believe me *knocking* is an understatement – I'm surprised there wasn't structural damage. I was sure this whole misunderstanding could be sorted out if only Daniel would speak to me – I just wasn't sure how to get him to do that. This was definitely a relationship emergency that required some serious female advice.

'Daniel's mad about you,' Seema reassured me as we got changed for PE. Seema is so brilliant at times like this. 'All relationships go through rocky patches.' I really think she should become an agony aunt. 'Honestly, I don't suppose you've got anything to feel jealous about.'

'Jealous?' I couldn't believe what I was hearing. And Seema calls herself my friend?

'Yes, Madge – you know that jolly green giant,

32

Jealousy,' Arlette chipped in. Which makes me think that she isn't actually over Daniel herself.

'What me? Jealous of Kara Kennedy? As if!'

Just then Ms Bignell blew the whistle. 'Year 9s!' she said in her dainty little voice. 'We're going to double up this morning with Miss Crumm's group and have an inter-form rounders tournament.'

Brilliant! No, honestly – I love rounders, mainly because I couldn't hit the ball if it was the size of an elephant so I'm always out first innings and then I can sit on the grass with my mates. And when it's our turn to field, I make sure I'm First Deep, so that I can sit on the grass behind first base where no one ever hits it. We'd won the toss and Candy Meekin, our captain, had opted to field first, which was nice because it meant I could have a rest after all the trauma of the morning.

'Magenta Orange!' Uh-oh, it was The Rhino. 'Perhaps you have mistaken the rounders pitch for a holiday camp – stand up!'

But then my nightmares really started. First in to bat was only Tennis the Menace, Kara Kennedy, who:

a) has a forehand drive like an honorary Williams sister and

b) is left-handed!

Which means she whacks the ball about half a mile

every time *and* they go straight to First Deep! So much for my cushy lesson making daisy chains and catching up on all the goss! And then, just to make my day six zillion times worse, after she'd made me run the equivalent of a half marathon in one lesson, Kara Kennedy came up to me in the changing rooms.

'Hi, Magenta.'

There was no way I was going to give her the satisfaction of thinking I was a bad loser so I smiled. 'Hello, Kara. Well played.'

She had this sickly grin on her face like a cat that had just brought up a fur ball. 'It's so nice that there's no hard feelings,' she gloated. 'Some people turn really bitchy when they see someone else going out with their ex.'

Huh? Ex? Until that point I thought Daniel and I had simply had a bit of a misunderstanding.

Before I could say anything she gave this smirk and put her head on one side as though she was being sympathetic. 'Hasn't he told you yet? Daniel's so sensitive, he's probably thinking of a way to let you down gently. He's so sweet, isn't he? I don't know how you could two-time him but then, your loss is my good fortune.' I was speechless – I know, but there's a first time for everything! Then she went on, 'Will you still be going bowling tomorrow night, now you're on your own? I'd offer you a lift in my mum's car but I'd hate you to feel uncomfortable with Daniel and me. You know what they say about three being a crowd.'

I was gobsmacked! And that's how it happened. 'Actually,' I said, 'I'm not on my own.'

'Really?' Kara raised her eyebrows – like she didn't believe me, or something. 'So who's the lucky boy, Magenta?'

I was just about to invent some fictitious boyfriend from another school when I had a brainwave! OK, so I know some of my brainwaves have landed me in pretty scary predicaments in the past but this one was pure genius.

'Sam Pudmore,' I said. Spud's fancied me for ages so it was a fairly safe bet that he'd agree to go bowling with me. And, like I said, he's looking kinda hot these days – well, lukewarm anyway, which is definitely a step in the right direction.

Kara Kennedy smirked. 'Spud? Really?'

'Yes, really!' I said.

'I must congratulate him.' As she walked out of the changing room, she gave this sneer. 'I'll look forward to tomorrow night then. Ciao!'

Seema and Arlette were both looking at me as though I'd suddenly morphed into a five-eyed alien.

'Spud?'

'Seriously?'

'Trust me,' I reassured them. 'I know what Daniel's playing at. He thinks he can get me jealous by going out with Sporty Spice Mark Two. Well, he can think again. I'm not interested in someone who's that pathetic. Spud is kind and considerate and he would never treat me the way Daniel's treated me.'

'Well, you did snog Chad Albright,' Arlette pointed out.

Er, hello! A severe bout of selective memory syndrome, I think!

'IT WAS FOR CHARITY!' I shouted and stomped off to find Spud before Kara Kennedy could get her enormously muscly hands on him.

4
Magenta

Did I say Spud was looking kinda hot? Well, rewind. He only went and turned up at the bowling centre wearing a flowery shirt, lime-green tie and white trainers! Talk about a fashion nightmare!

'Hi, Magenta.' He gave this gormless grin and smoothed down his tie. 'I wanted to dress up for you on our first proper date.'

Dress up? As what – Austin Powers? 'Wow,' I managed. 'You look . . . er . . .'

But before I could finish, Bruno, the youth leader, came round collecting our money and doing a head count. 'OK – listen up, folks. Once I've paid you can collect your bowling shoes and then get into groups of four people per lane. When you've finished bowling you can use the slot machines or the food hall. Georgie and I will be around so, let's go and enjoy ourselves.'

'OK, four people.' I turned to Seema and Arlette but then realised that they were with Hayden West and Ben Jestico. Oh no! I was going to have to choose between my two best friends – or ask them to ditch their boyfriends. What a mate crisis!

But then I heard Spud yell, 'Yo! Angus, dude!' Dude? Who says *dude* these days? 'Why don't you and Chelsea come and make up a foursome with me and Magenta?'

I was in shock. 'Like, hello! Don't you think you should ask me before you invite that social deadwood to join us?'

Spud shrugged. 'Angus is my best mate.'

Which, if you go with my dad's theory of *you-are-judged-by-the-people-you-hang-with*, was more than a teensy bit worrying.

'For one thing,' I challenged, 'I thought that skunk Daniel was supposed to be your best mate. And for another, did the whole social deadwood factor go over your head?'

Spud raised his chin and did this slicing motion across his throat, like he'd suddenly joined the Mafia. 'Me and Daniel are history, man!' It was as though he'd had this sudden injection of machismo. And, to be ruthlessly honest, it didn't really fit with the floral shirt and ponytail – which was now starting to look way too girly for an Indie bass player. But, on the positive side, at least he'd soon be able to dump the white trainers for bowling shoes. I never thought I'd see the day when I thought bowling shoes would improve someone's image.

And then I heard this deep laughter rolling across the foyer. I looked up and Chad Albright was walking through the door with a group of girls from Year 10. He was wearing this white tracksuit with a navy stripe down it and the letters C.I.A. across the back. And he had a navy blue baseball cap turned back to front. Ohmigod! He looked sooooo gorgeous.

'Wow!' I said, without thinking. 'Is Chad Albright in the CIA?'

'Nooo!' Spud sounded a teensy bit put out. Oops! Maybe he wasn't the best person to ask about Chad in view of the fact that I'd chosen Chad over him in the unmentionable game show incident. 'His middle name is *Indiana*,' he said in a phoney American accent. Wow! Indiana for a middle name, how Hollywood is that? But Spud was really peed off. 'If you'd rather have come bowling with him, why did you ask me?'

Hmm! Now that *was* a good question. And, to be honest, I couldn't think of an answer – other than a temporary loss of rational thought in the face of extreme pressure from Kara Kennedy. 'I asked you . . . er . . . because . . .' I looked Spud up and down, hoping for some sort of inspiration. 'Because you're . . .' I peered over his shoulder and checked out Chad who was standing with his legs apart and his hands in his pockets looking soooooo cool. 'Because you're . . . er . . . interesting,' I finished.

Spud seemed to grow about two inches and his chest puffed out like a pigeon. 'Wow!' he grinned. 'No one's ever called me interesting before.'

Phew! That was a close one. So, having restored my date's ego, I now had the knotty little problem of the lane sharing to solve.

Am I a genius, or am I a genius? It just took a little bit of lateral thinking to come up with a solution – girls versus boys! Me, Seema, Arlette and Chelsea in one lane, against Spud, Hayden, Ben and Angus in the next one. How brilliant am I? Only from the look on Ben and Hayden's faces, I got the distinct impression that they thought they'd drawn the short straw.

'Oh get over it, Hayden. Just look at it as widening your social circle,' I said. Sometimes people can be so negative.

There was another teensy bit of a hitch when we got to our lanes, though. We'd thought we would be able to get two lanes in the same booth so that we could all be together but we discovered that we'd been allocated lanes where the seating areas backed on to each other rather than ones that shared a console. Which, to be honest, was a bit irritating – especially as we were facing a family who looked like a pack of pugs (you know, those dogs with squashed faces that old ladies carry about under their arms). The boys seemed happy, though; they were sharing with the Albright groupies and were ogling them like they hadn't seen girls before.

'Oh get over it, Magenta,' Hayden mimicked. 'We're just widening our social circle.' Ggggrrr!

However, *not* being a person to dwell on negativity myself, I wasn't going to let it bother me. We could still talk and compare scores across the back of the seats. But, even though I am generally very positive, the next hiccough of the evening did really start to pee me off. It seemed that the bowling ball I'd picked (I'd chosen this really gorgeous pink one that went with my top) had something wrong with it. Whereas everyone else's trundled down the wooden lane like they're supposed to, mine had a preferred route of veering off to the left and rolling along the gutter. By the time we'd played three frames, I hadn't knocked down a single pin. And it didn't help hearing all the cheers coming from the next booth where, every time Chad Albright scored a strike, he did a victory punch in the air and his little gang of followers clapped and whooped like a day trip from kindergarten. How nauseatingly immature are they? I was just giving them the evil eye when Spud leaned over the back of the bench.

'Your hips and shoulders should face forwards when you release the ball,' he said. 'You're letting your shoulder come across, that's why it's going over that way.' Cheek!

'It isn't me,' I protested. 'It's the ball. I think it's weighted.' Plus, although I didn't say this to Spud, I'd allowed myself to get momentarily distracted by Chad and his band of merry maniacs.

'Let me show you.' And he came round to our lane and started putting his arms round me from the back like he was giving some sort of master class.

'Whoa!' I straightened up and moved away from him. 'Back off! What do you think you're doing?'

He went bright red (which so clashed with his shirt and tie). 'Sorry, Magenta. I was only trying to help. My dad's in a team and I've been coming bowling since I was a kid.'

'Maybe you need a different ball,' suggested Seema, which is what I call true friendship.

'No, I think it's more to do with her action,' Spud said, which got up my nose on two counts:

1) he was talking about me like I wasn't there and,

2) he seemed determined to make it *my* fault that the ball wouldn't go where it was supposed to.

'Good idea, Seema,' I said pointedly.

But then this awful thing happened – when I went to the ball rack, I realised that the next size was a hideous yellow colour that looked totally gross against my top. What a dilemma! Maybe, if I didn't hold it too close to my body, no one would notice the grotesque colour scheme.

'Hey! Gerroff! That's my ball!' shrieked this little girl who was part of the Pug Family in the next lane. And she made a grab for it.

'There's no such thing as ownership of the bowling balls,' I said, snatching it back from her.

Then Mr Pug, who quite frankly made Homer Simpson look like Mr Universe, stood up. 'Oi! What d'you think you're doing?'

'It's all right, sir,' Spud said, stepping in between Pug Daddy and me – you see, he can be quite sweet sometimes. 'My girlfriend just needs to use it for one bowl.'

Girlfriend? Obviously Spud had been overdosing on the wishing-toffee again. I thought I'd made it very clear that this was a one-off date for the sole purpose of avoiding the potential ruination of my social life caused by Daniel – although when I look at Spud's dress sense, perhaps there'd have been significantly less damage to my reputation if I'd come on my own.

'Don't cry, princess. You can have the ball back in a minute, babe,' Mr Pug was saying. 'Let's order you a drink.'

Phew! Another crisis averted. Now to show Spud that it actually wasn't my fault that the ball wouldn't roll straight. I placed my fingers in the holes, and held up the ball, lining it with the centre pin (and taking care not to place it too close to my pink top). I was going to show him that I wasn't totally useless. I stepped forward and brought my arm back the way the poster in the foyer told me to do it. Then, as I brought my arm through ready to release the ball, I heard Angus Lyle shout, 'Yo! Danno! Over here!'

Daniel? Oh no! I thought he'd decided not to come because of his plaster. I spun round and there was the Rodent King himself holding hands with Ms Fitness Freak. I gave a jolt of horror, which swivelled my hips and shoulders and meant they were not facing straight, the way Spud had said they should. Then my foot slithered forwards on the newly polished wood so that I sank into this sort of bent-knee version of the splits as I let go of the ball.

'Owww!' I wailed, as my wrist twisted round,

almost jerking my thumb out of its socket. The ball was propelled upwards before it crashed down with a thud and trickled into the gutter again.

'Are you all right, Magenta?' Spud ran up and put his arm round me. And this time I didn't move away. If Daniel wanted to make something of it, he could – see if I cared!

'My thumb,' I sobbed. 'It's broken.' And then I realised that the reason my thumb was throbbing so much was because the knuckle was swelling up where my thumb ring had been wrenched off. 'My ring!' I yelled. 'It's in the ball.' I stood up and was about to run after the grotesque yellow ball, when (as if my arm hadn't incurred enough damage for one evening) Spud caught hold of me and yanked me back. 'Aaaagh!' I screamed, as my shoulders went back and, once again, my bowling shoes slipped on the slippery floor. One minute I was upright and the next my feet were up above my head and I crashed down on to the wood.

Then, just to complete my total and utter humiliation, a klaxon sounded and a voice came over the Tannoy. 'This is a customer announcement – would the players in lane ten stay *behind* the foul line.'

Humiliation alert! Everyone (including Chad and

45

his gaggle of groupies) was staring at me. At that moment I wished I could just rumble into the gutter myself so that the pinsetter would sweep me away into oblivion.

'Are you OK?' Spud asked.

'You mean apart from the terminal embarrassment of being rugby tackled in the middle of a bowling alley?' I snapped.

'Sorry, Magenta.' At least he had the decency to look shamefaced. 'But look, your ball's come round again!'

Sure enough, the pukey yellow ball came trundling along the tracks towards us and rolled up on to the rack. I was just about to pick it up and retrieve my ring when the pug grub only went and grabbed it right out of my hands.

'Hey – that's my ball!' I shouted, reaching out and taking it from her.

'My turn!' she yelled, wrapping her arms round it and pulling it to her chest.

Then her father piped up. 'You've been nothing but trouble since you arrived, now give it back.'

'Look,' I said, being extremely reasonable. 'I don't want to use it.' I made to grab the ball again. 'I just want my ring back.' And I put both my hands round the ball and yanked it backwards out of her grip.

'Let go!' shouted Father Pug.

And, not realising that he'd actually been talking to me, his moron daughter released her grip just as I snatched the ball up out of her hands. Yes! But my moment of triumph was short-lived. The momentum of pulling the ball from the girl propelled me backwards and, with the bowling ball above my head, I overbalanced, toppling into the waiter who was bringing a tray of drinks to Team Pug. As he careered to one side, the tray of drinks went up in the air, depositing its contents all down the waiter and catching one or two of the Pug Family in its wash as well. Amazingly though, I managed to escape without a single drop hitting me.

'I've had enough of that girl,' bellowed the father. 'She's been disrupting our game all evening.'

Durr! Can you believe the man? But apparently my so-called date did! Spud began pulling my sleeve in the direction of the food hall. 'Come on, Magenta,' he said, 'let's go for a Coke.'

'What!' I yelled as Spud dragged me away from my mates. 'That is *so* unfair!'

'See you later, Madge,' called Seema and Arlette. To be honest, I'd expected a little more support from them too.

And I still hadn't found my thumb ring. Although,

when you think about it, it's probably for the best. It'd been a present from Daniel and I really should remove all trace of him from my life. Make a totally new start. Yes, that's what I was going to do. In fact, I couldn't have cared less if my ring had gone – who needs stupid reminders anyway? See what I mean about being a positive person? I can always find the silver lining to any cloud.

Unfortunately, when we got to the cafeteria area, the devious duo themselves were only sitting at a table by the window. And Kara had a truly geeky bandana round her head. I mean, they are so nerdy – I don't know what Daniel sees in her. Of course he wasn't allowed to bowl because of his plaster but I knew what his game was. He'd only turned up to try and make me jealous. Well, it wasn't going to work.

'Let's go and play pool,' I suggested to Spud, doing a hundred and eighty degree turn and marching him out of the cafeteria again.

The games section was right next to the food hall and there were several pool tables surrounded by arcade machines. I'd never played pool before so Spud offered to give me lessons which, in theory, seemed like a sweet thing to do but, in reality, was actually annoying because he started talking to me as though I was about six.

'OK, so see how I'm holding my cue?' he said in this really patronising voice. 'Now you do it. All right?' Durr! It was soooo not all right! How difficult was it to hold a stick of wood? 'Now glide it forward and don't whack the ball, just knock it gently.'

Spud leaned over me from behind and reached his arm over my cue. Which, I've got to be honest, was a bit too close for my liking, but I didn't say anything. I just hoped Daniel was clocking an eyeful.

'OK.' As I pushed my cue forwards, I looked up, just to check that Daniel had seen Spud and me getting up close and personal, but I could hardly believe my eyes! Daniel was leaning over his pizza and kissing Kara Kennedy – on the lips. And not like it was a mercy-snog either. It went on for ages and ages like they were on some sort of snog-fest world record attempt or something. The slimy pond-life! It was only three days since we'd been going out and now he was playing tonsil tennis with Nelly Netball.

I rammed my cue towards the pool ball – but oops! There was a sickening ripping sound.

'Jeez, Magenta! Look what you've done!' Spud's eyes were out on stalks like he couldn't believe what he was seeing. Instead of hitting the ball, my cue had slipped sideways and gouged a lump out of the blue baize that covered the table.

'It's just a little tear,' I pleaded. 'No one'll notice. Come on, carry on teaching me,' I said, taking Spud's arm and trying to wrap it round me again so that, if Daniel was looking over in our direction, he'd realise what he was missing.

But I've never seen Spud so agitated. 'Are you serious? It costs hundreds to get a pool table re-covered. Let's get out of here before anyone sees.'

His arms were flapping about like an octopus on Pepsi Max. He went to grab the cue from me but to be honest, I was getting a teensy bit sick of people grabbing things off me tonight.

'I want to play,' I said, snatching the cue back, but it flew out of my hand and did this amazing cheerleader-type twirl in the air. The trouble was, it cracked down over the head of this huge boy with a shaved head and about fifty-seven earrings in each ear, who was standing next to that machine where you feed in coins to try and make them drop over the edge.

'Owwww!' He keeled sideways into the machine and began rubbing his head. Then there was the sound of money tumbling on to the floor and suddenly sirens started going off. The boy picked up the cue then spun round and started scouring the pool tables. When he saw me he lurched forwards.

'You little . . .' But before he could finish, security guards had descended from all quarters. 'I'll get you!' he shouted at me as they wrestled him to the floor.

'No jogging the machines,' yelled one of the bouncers. And they frogmarched him out of the building.

I turned to Spud. 'Phew, that was a close one.'

Spud shook his head. 'Erm, I'm not sure it's that simple, Magenta. Look.' He pointed towards the glass doors. I could see the boy pacing up and down the car park and mouthing things in my direction and, although I can't lip-read, I was pretty sure he wasn't paying me compliments.

'Ooo! He doesn't look very happy. Do you think I should go and explain to the manager that it was an accident and it wasn't really his fault?'

Spud looked at me with this really yucky smile. 'Oh, you're so sweet, Magenta.'

Just then Daniel limped over. 'Are you OK? I saw what happened.'

Oh yes! That meant that he must have been watching *me* while he was kissing Kara Kennedy. And it's so *not* true passion if your eyes are open – I read it in a magazine.

'We're fine!' Spud said, his smile suddenly disappearing.

But then Daniel looked shocked. 'Jeez! What the hell happened to the pool table?'

Honestly – why are boys so negative? I was just about to explain, when Spud and Daniel decided they were all lads together again. So much for them being history.

'We're in one big pile of poo here, Danno,' Spud said. His eyes were flashing from left to right like he was planning some army-style manoeuvres. 'This is the situation . . .' And then he started talking about me like I wasn't there again. 'Problemo numero uno – there's a gorilla with a sore head waiting for her outside, comprendez?' And he nodded towards the door. 'Problemo numero dos – if the management find her she's probably going to get landed with a bill for the pool table, not to mention what Bruno's going to say.'

'Whoa!' I said, feeling justifiably affronted by all this Euro-babble that was being spoken about me.

But Daniel only put up his hand to shush me! Can you believe it? And he's not even my boyfriend. 'I've got an idea,' he said, leaning forward and pushing the pool balls into a cluster, covering the tear. 'Now, let's move slowly back into the cafeteria as though nothing's happened.'

'Er, hello! Don't I get a say in this?' I asked, not

particularly wanting to spend the rest of the evening with Caustic Kara.

'Not at the moment,' Daniel said. 'Just walk casually and do as I say.'

Which just confirmed that dumping him was the right move – he is so bossy.

Getting back to the food hall seemed to take for ever because Daniel was still hobbling at the speed of your average geriatric snail, but when we got there Kara Kennedy was only sitting at the table with Chad Albright and his band of happy clappy followers.

She put on this obviously fake smile. 'Have you heard of the Chaos Theory, Chad? That's the one where Magenta flutters her eyelashes and the whole of Europe collapses into a black hole.'

Meeeeow! 'Well at least when I flutter my eyelashes, they're all my own and not stick-ons,' I retorted.

'Girls!' Daniel said, like he'd suddenly gone from fourteen to forty in one millisecond. 'Kara take off your head scarf and give it to Magenta.'

'Eeww! No way!' Kara and I both said together.

'I am not wearing a bandana – they are so last millennium,' I pointed out.

'It is *not* a bandana – it's a head wrap,' Kara said. 'And there's no way I'm letting *her* touch it.'

Just then Spud prodded Daniel in the ribs. 'Hey, don't look now but there's a bouncer coming this way.'

Eeek! Sure enough there was a man the size of Godzilla walking from the pool table towards the food hall and he was making straight for our group.

'Quick! Put it on,' Daniel said, snatching Kara's head wrap and handing it to me. 'And now the jacket.'

'What?' Kara looked shocked. I have to say, I wasn't too pleased myself. Not that there was anything wrong with the jacket – it was quite a nice knitted jacket, actually, but it was in this dark green which so did not go with my pink top.

'Just do it,' Daniel said – pretty forcefully, I have to say. I didn't know what his plan was but I didn't like the look of that bouncer, so I quickly put on Kara's headband and cardigan. 'Now,' Daniel continued, 'Chad, you take Magenta out of the door at the far side so that the guy waiting outside doesn't see her.' He looked at me. 'Magenta, no one's going to recognise you if you're wearing different clothes and you're with Chad.'

I looked from Chad to Spud. No, there was no similarity whatsoever. Which brought me back to the question of why I'd asked Spud to go bowling in the first place and not Chad?

'I'll get everyone else together and meet you over by the minibus in ten minutes. OK – go!' Daniel said.

How exciting was that? Being sneaked out under cover by Chad *Indiana* Albright. It was soooo James Bond. I was even beginning to think that Daniel wasn't so bad after all and, maybe if I went round and tried to explain about the whole charity thing we could get back together, but then he only went and let the cat out of the bag about the pool table to my dad. Now I am grounded for a whole week. It's only because it's my SATs next week and Dad's freaking out that I'll do as badly as I did in the mocks. Mind you, on the positive side, I've got the perfect excuse not to go out with Spud again. You see – there's always a silver lining.

5
Daniel

This is not how I'd wanted things to go at all. I mean, don't get me wrong, Kara's really nice and everything. She's pretty and she can be funny sometimes and she's clever and, like Magnus says, she looks really hot in her tennis skirt. In fact, all the boys fancy her (except Perry Proctor from the Portakabin Crew and he's definitely two sandwiches short of a picnic). So, it's not that there's anything wrong with Kara. It's just that . . . she's not Magenta.

I mean, last week at bowling everything was going OK. Even though I couldn't bowl because of my leg, I was looking forward to seeing everyone again. Apart from that one fateful afternoon during Charity Week, I haven't been in school since before Easter. Anyway, we got there a bit later than everyone else because Kara's mum gave us a lift and she had to get petrol on the way. The minute we walked through the door Angus shouted to me.

'Yo! Danno! Over here!'

It was great to be there with all the gang again. I gave him the thumbs-up and was just about to go over there to join the lads, when my eyes drifted over to the next lane. And there she was: a vision in pink, with these really cute little bowling shoes on her feet. And just at that minute, she did this dainty little skid so that she ended up sitting in the middle of the lane – oh, she looked so gorgeous. I wanted to rush over to her and take her in my arms and lift her on to her feet again and promise to look after her for ever (but, I still had my plaster on at that stage, so rushing wasn't really an option). Instead, Spud (my treacherous, former best mate) was all over her like the measles while I could only stand and watch and pretend that I didn't care.

'Later, Angus!' I called over, then turned to Kara. 'Let's go and get something to eat.'

How sad was I? Bottling out of hanging with my mates because of a girl? And when Kara and I went to have a pizza, I looked across at Magenta and I thought of my mum's words the previous evening.

'Daniel, have you noticed that this seems to be becoming a habit with you? Going out with girls even though your heart isn't in it?'

My mum's chosen bedtime reading is *Kitchen-Sink Psychology for Dummies*! She thinks we should all be on a voyage of self-discovery. The trouble is, my voyage seems to be more towards the bottom of the sea, slowly drowning in all these feelings that leave me totally useless half the time. But, the scary thing about my mum and her amateur analysis sessions, is that she's usually right. I mean, look at what she'd just said – it was true; Arlette, Magenta's cousin Justine, Hattie Pringle – all of them really nice girls but all of them just fill-ins until Magenta saw fit to go out with me again.

'Can you honestly say you're happy?' She was standing at the end of my bed with her arms piled up with clean washing and her emotion-detector on full alert. 'Is this how you want your life to be, Daniel?'

OK, I'd got the picture: my mother thought I was a desperate, spineless loser when it came to the female of the species. 'No, Mum,' I'd said, staring up at Sarah Michelle and feeling like the plaster on my leg had ridden up and was crushing my heart.

'Mooching about and just going out with any girl who asks you?'

'No, Mum.' What did she think I was going to say: *Actually, Mother, that's exactly how I want my life to pan out*?

'Or are you going to take control of your life now?' My mum's a nurse and she went on a positive thinking course last month to try to improve patient recovery. If this was her idea of a pep talk, I think the death toll on her ward is about to rise sharply.

'Yes, Mum.' I thought that if I just kept agreeing with her, she'd go away and congratulate herself on a job well done.

'Are you actually listening to me, Daniel, or are you just saying this to keep me quiet in the hope that I'll go away and leave you in peace?'

Oh God! She really is a member of the thought police. 'No, I am listening,' I lied.

'Good.' She dumped the washing on the end of the bed. 'It's time you stopped moping about, Daniel. I know it's hard living next door to Magenta when you still have feelings for her, but there's an old song you might want to listen to. It goes something like, if you can't be with the one you love, then love the one you're with.' What was that supposed to mean? She hovered in the doorway, like she was going to say something else, but then thought better of it. Actually, she's been doing a lot of that recently. 'Good night, love.' She kissed me on the forehead and left – like she hadn't just destroyed every last gram of self-esteem in my body.

So, there I was, looking over my pizza at Kara Kennedy, and I thought, *Daniel, you've either got to shape up or ship out. Stop mooning about over Magenta.*

You're with a really cool girl, so make the most of it.
And I leaned over and kissed her – just like that. It
was all right. You know, no fireworks or anything.
No starburst rockets going off inside me. But it was
OK. And then I looked over Kara's shoulder and
there was Magenta, leaning over the pool table
looking so lovely as she tried to shoot some pool –
except that Spud (middle name Judas) had his arm
wrapped right round her. He might as well have
picked up the cue and whacked it straight through
my heart.

'Wow, Daniel, that was amazing,' Kara was saying,
going all gooey.

But I couldn't take my eyes off Magenta. 'Cheers,
mate,' I said distractedly. And I must admit, she gave
me a bit of a weird look.

Then there was this huge commotion over by
the machines and a guy with a face like an iguana
seemed to be on the verge of attacking Magenta –
poor, sweet, Magenta. Kara's lips were moving, but I
wasn't hearing her. All I could see was Magenta
looking afraid and vulnerable and Spud standing
there like a pilchard. And then Mum's little talk
kicked in. Was I going to carry on acting like a
spineless loser or was I going to take control of my
life and leap over there to protect the girl of my

dreams? OK, well, maybe leaping was a bit out of the question as there was more of a resemblance to Tortoise Man than Superman, but still – I limped to her rescue, like a true knight in shining leg-armour.

Spud was a bit off with me at first, but he's an OK guy underneath and, to give him his due, he has fancied Magenta for almost as long as I have. Although, I'm beginning to think that his parents' decision to give him extra Spanish tuition was a bit of a no-no.

Anyway, to cut a not so long story even shorter and not wanting to brag too much about my brilliance, I hatched this amazingly cunning plan to smuggle Magenta out of the bowling alley. The only downside being that I had to use Chad (The Floss-meister) Albright as a decoy. I'd have given anything to do it myself but I knew my broken leg was a bit of a giveaway. Magenta seemed really grateful afterwards and I was sure there might be a glimmer of hope for us to get together again. But then motormouth moron me only went and blew it at the weekend.

Curtis, Magenta's dad, and Belinda had come round to talk to Mum about their wedding because Mum's going to make the wedding cake for them.

I'd wandered – sorry, hobbled – into the living

room in the hope that I might get a nanosecond on my own to use the PS2 while my sabre-toothed sibling was out doing his Saturday job at the minimart, but there was a full-scale wedding briefing going on.

'So, Mary, are you sure you're OK with that?' Belinda used to be an Art teacher at our school until she left at Easter. She's really cool and she was holding up this amazing drawing of a cake that looked a bit like a floral Taj Mahal. 'You'll be able to get all the ingredients at the health food shop but it's very important that they're all organic and vegan.'

'Sure, Belinda, that won't be a problem,' Mum was saying, looking more than a tad anxious as she eyed Belinda's diagram. 'And what about icing?'

'We've decided against icing as such, so it'll be covered in organic marzipan with the flower decorations in melted carob.'

'Wonderful,' Mum said, less than convincingly.

Then Curtis spoke to me. 'Hello, Daniel. How're you doing? Your mum tells me your cast's coming off next week. I bet you're itching to get rid of it.'

Why do adults do that – state the blatantly obvious? What was I meant to say? Actually, Curtis, I'll be sad to see it go; I've grown really fond of the old plaster of Paris leg attire and was thinking of making it a permanent feature – so much warmer than socks – except for the round-the-toe area!

But, of course, I didn't say that. Dropping the Mr Nice-guy image is pretty hard to do after fourteen years. So instead I made a joke. 'Itching's the right word – it's driving me nuts at the moment.' They gave me this pitying smile and then I couldn't stand it any longer. Against all my better judgement my mouth performed a military coup on my brain and just blurted out the question I'd been dying to ask since the previous night. 'How's Magenta?'

As soon as I'd said it, I knew it was a mistake.

'She's fine, thank you,' Curtis said, giving Belinda a sideways glance. 'How was bowling last night?'

And from the way he said it, I assumed (like any normal person would who knows what parents are like) that they knew what had happened. Oh boy, was that a big mistake!

'It wasn't Magenta's fault, you know. She just slipped and . . .'

Well, I'm sure you can imagine the rest.

Later that night, as I was lying on my bed and watching the portable television my dad bought me as a get well present when I broke my leg, there was this pounding on my French window like Demolition Woman with a sledgehammer.

'Daniel! I know you're in there, so don't even bother trying to hide.' I knew I should've closed my blind. 'You pathetic pond-life, how could you? Come out here this minute.'

Oh yeah! Like that was going to entice me on to my balcony! As much as I love Magenta it would be like committing very messy hara-kiri. I don't think I've ever heard her that angry.

'Thanks to you I'm grounded for a whole week, so the least you could do is make some feeble attempt to explain yourself.'

Which I thought was fair comment – not that I had any intention of doing it face to face. Call me a wuss, but I value my life.

'I'm sorry. It just slipped out,' I called from the safety of my bed. And even I had to admit, it sounded lame.

'It slipped out?' she screeched. 'Slipped out? What happened? Did my dad ask you if you'd enjoyed yourself and you said, yes thank you I had a brilliant time and Magenta clobbered this Neanderthal with a cue and ripped up the pool table?'

How uncanny is that? 'Yes!' I shouted through the glass. 'That's exactly how it happened.'

'You know what, Daniel, I can always tell when you're lying,' she screamed. 'Because your lips are moving!'

So I'm going to do what my mum suggested. I certainly can't be with the one I love at the moment – or ever again from the way Magenta stomped off back to her own bedroom – so I have no choice but to love the one I'm with. Kara Kennedy is now officially my girlfriend and Magenta is banished from my mind – for ever. I will never speak of her or even think of her again – ever.

And another thing – I noticed that she'd taken off the thumb ring I bought her as a 'thank you for being such a wonderful girlfriend' present. But that's the very last thing I'm going to say about her. We are so over. As from now, not another word.

I can hear her banging around in her room. And now it sounds as though she's crying. Oh, poor Magenta – I wonder if I should go round there and see if she's all right?

OK, OK! I know what I said – no more Mr Nice-guy. That is definitely it! Magenta is history.

6
Arlette

I am so excited – I can't wait till we go to camp. I've been looking forward to it since the notice first went up in September. It'll be so brilliant. I know Magenta isn't too keen, in fact, she says that the phrase 'outdoor living' is a contradiction in terms, but I hope that once she's there she'll change her mind.

Although, maybe not. Because, whereas Seema and I are really looking forward to the whole experience and just wishing that our boyfriends could be there to make it even better, Madge can't think of a single good thing about camp in the first place and the fact that her boyfriend *will* be there is making it seem a hundred and fifty-nine times worse! Of course, whether or not she and Spud make it till then is a whole different matter.

Take last week – we were sitting in the quad talking about our SATs. Hayden and Ben had come over and Seema was offering round her crisps. 'You know that question on writing to inform, explain or describe?' she said to no one in particular. 'Well, I chose the one about writing an article for the local paper and I've been thinking about when we have our career interviews next week, I'd quite like to go into journalism you know. Or – better still – media journalism.'

'I thought you wanted to be a scientist?' said Madge.

'Or a musician?' I queried. Honestly, Seema has so many choices, it's just not fair.

'I could always be a scientific journalist,' she said. 'And do my music as a hobby.'

Hayden snatched her hairbrush out of her bag and held it up like a microphone. 'This is ace reporter, Seema Karia, for Sky News outside Archimedes High, where it's just been proved that extraterrestrial intelligence is an oxymoron. And to prove it, we have an alien with only half a brain cell.' He turned and pushed the hairbrush at Spud. 'Do you have anything to say to the viewers?'

'Hey, who're you calling an oxymoron?' Spud said, looking a bit miffed.

'I rest my case,' Hayden laughed.

I have to admit, I wasn't totally sure what an oxymoron was myself. I remember talking about them in English and I seem to recall it's something along the same lines as Madge's 'outdoor living' but I wasn't a hundred per cent certain.

Seema gave Hayden a playful slap on the arm. 'Don't be so horrible. Leave Spud alone.'

But Magenta flapped her hand. 'Nah! Spud doesn't mind, do you?'

'Well—' Spud began.

'See,' Madge interrupted. 'It's just a bit of fun.'

I took one of Seema's crisps. 'I did the question about writing a brochure and I did it about the summer camp,' I said. 'It was so cool, I was listing all these things like horse-riding and canoeing and rock-climbing.'

Magenta looked at me like *I* was the extraterrestrial with only half a brain cell. 'Arl,' she said, 'how can the words horse-riding, canoeing and rock-climbing possibly feature in the same sentence as cool?'

I was starting to feel a bit miffed because it didn't matter how hard I tried to drum up some enthusiasm for camp, Madge seemed determined to put a downer on it. 'Well I think they're cool.'

'Yeah, right! In the land of tweed socks and hairy knees.'

'Well, rock-climbing can be cool if you climb high enough. Boom, boom!' Spud did an imaginary drum roll ending with a pretend crash on air cymbals. 'And, if you fall out of the canoe that can also be very coo—'

'Spud!' Madge snapped.

I know Spud's jokes are cornier than a family-sized packet of cornflakes, but I thought she was a bit off with him. In fact, she's been off with him since the Science test earlier in the week. Actually, that's not strictly true; she's been off with him since way before that – she's been off with him since – well, for ever really! But the Science test definitely didn't help. Most of us have learned that, in the interest of our own safety, it's best not to discuss tests with Madge. All it does is upset her when she realises she's got completely the wrong end of the stick again, but poor old Spud went wading in with his size twenty-four wellies.

'No, no, no, Magenta. Proteins are completely different from protons. Protons are the positively charged particles in an atom and proteins—'

'Whoa there, Johnny Neurone.' Magenta stopped him, mid-explanation. 'First of all, if there's that much difference, they should change more than a couple of letters. And secondly, if I'd wanted to go out with Einstein, I'd have contacted a medium.'

'A medium what? Boom, boom!' he'd asked – which really didn't help his case.

'Oh my God! You are sooo doing my brain in!'

I think that was the second (or was it the third?)

time Magenta dumped Spud – and that's only been this week! But, back to the conversation about camp:

'Sorry, Magenta,' Spud said. 'But I'm with Arlette on this. I'm really looking forward to camp. Hey hey!' He put two thumbs up to me. 'It's only just after half term. Not long now!'

'Not long enough,' Magenta grumbled. Honestly, I know she's my best friend but sometimes she can be so negative.

Just then, we heard this commotion over by the sports hall and when we looked over, Chad Albright had come out wearing his basketball kit. You should've seen him – he was really posing by the drinking fountain and all these Year 10 girls were swarming round him like flies round a compost heap. And just to prove my point, there in the middle of them was Anthea Pritchard, the biggest slapper in the school.

'Huh!' Magenta said, looking daggers at her. 'Can you believe it? The Pritch is only making a play for Chad. Mind you,' she said, 'she's had all my cast-offs.'

'Er, hello!' I pointed out. 'The only boy Anthea's gone out with after you was Ryan Dunn and you said yourself, you were better off without him. She was going out with Adam Jordan *before* you had your one and only date with him and you can hardly call Chad Albright one of your cast-offs – it was one kiss!'

'A charity kiss,' Magenta prompted.

'If you say so.' I looked at Spud who was looking distinctly hurt with all this talk of Chad Albright. 'Anyway,' I went on, 'I always think it's better to concentrate on what you've got in life rather than wishing for something else.' Which is so true. I gave Ben a little squeeze as I said it. I mean, Ben's lovely and we've been going out for nearly six months now, which is practically a lifetime, but I've got to be honest, if Daniel Davis asked me out again, I'd go out with him like a shot. He is so the most gorgeous boy in the entire school. And, actually, I'm really annoyed that Magenta has had so many chances with Daniel and she's blown it every time. She just doesn't know when she's well off.

'Oh yeah! Concentrate on what I've got – like what?' she said.

'Ah hem.' Spud cleared his throat. Although Spud's not my type, he can be quite sweet sometimes. He's tying his hair back now, too, which means he's not as grungy looking – and I'm sure he'll grow into his ears soon.

Magenta looked at him. 'Something wrong, Spud?' He flicked his hair out of his eyes and winked at her.

'You got something in your eye? You should go to the nurse.'

But before Spud could say anything, Chad Albright walked over to our group and bounced shoulders with Spud. 'Hey, Spuddo. Good news, man. My dad's just been up to see the Head and told him he wants me to go to camp, so I'm gonna be tagging along with you guys.'

Spud looked a little taken aback. 'I thought all the places were taken?'

'I guess not.' I hate to admit this but, actually, his American accent is quite sexy.

'But Magnus Lyle didn't get picked and he was told that if anyone dropped out, he'd be the next on the waiting list.'

Chad shrugged. 'Not my problem, man. Say, Mr Snowdon's given me a kit list. He says there's a department store called Farrago with a camping department on the top floor. Fancy going on Saturday?'

Mr Snowdon's the boys' PE teacher and he's soooo gorgeous. He's going to be one of the male members of staff going to camp and it's about the only thing that Magenta finds remotely interesting about the entire week.

But with Chad's news she suddenly perked up.

'Ooo, I haven't bought any of my kit for camp yet.'

Chad gave her this weird smile. 'You're going to camp? Are you serious?'

She looked annoyed. 'And what's so funny about that?'

Chad shrugged. 'Nothing at all.' Only from the way he was trying not to laugh, it seemed that there was a lot that was funny about it. 'It's just that . . . how can I put it? Having seen your performance at the bowling alley, I didn't think physical pursuits were your strong point.'

'Oh believe me, Chad, you'd be surprised at my strong points. I have hidden talents,' Madge said and then she prodded me in the ribs and whispered, 'Did you hear that? He was watching me when we went bowling.' Only she said it like it was a good thing.

At which point Daniel limped over to our group. He's out of plaster now but he's still walking a bit strangely. At one point he thought he might not be able to go to camp but his physio says he should be OK by then. 'Has anyone seen Kara?' he asked. 'She was supposed to meet me at break.'

'No, sorry,' I said, squeezing up to Ben just in case Daniel might get a tiny bit jealous and decide that he wanted to go out with me again.

Magenta cupped her hand round her ear. 'Did somebody say something?'

Daniel raised his eyes and turned away but Chad stopped him. 'Hey, Danno! We're having a boys' afternoon at Farrago's on Saturday, buying our kit for camp. You up for it?'

Daniel stopped and seemed to be thinking about it, then he said, 'No thanks, Chad. I'm very particular about who I hang out with.'

'Wooooooo!' Hayden said.

And I must say, the way Daniel said it was so strong. Not horrible – just really straight to the point.

Chad reached forward and grabbed his sleeve to stop him leaving. 'Hey, listen, man. You're one of the good guys. I don't wanna fall out with you.'

'You should've thought of that before you kissed my girlfriend,' Daniel said without looking at Magenta.

Everyone went really quiet. It was getting juicy!

Chad held out his hands like he was appealing to Daniel's understanding side. 'Think about it, Danno. I was new to the school. I didn't know she was spoken for.'

Oops!

Magenta stood up. 'Er, hello! Two minor details: one – why does everyone keep talking about me like

I'm not here? And two, a point which everyone seems to have conveniently forgotten – it was for ch—!'

'Yeah, yeah, yeah! Whatever!' Daniel interrupted. Then he just walked away.

Magenta stood for about a minute with her mouth opening and closing like a goldfish at feeding time before she put her hands on her hips. 'Cheers, Chad – nice one!'

So, how is it, you might be asking, that Seema and I found ourselves on a stake-out with Magenta on the fourth floor of Farrago in the High Street on Saturday afternoon? Most other girls would've seen Chad for what he really is by now. But not Magenta! I don't know what it is with her and boys – it's like her boy-ometer is running on reverse current. The ones who are arrogant chauvinists like, I-love-myself-who-do-you-love Adam Jordan, Oscar-nominee-for-best-drama-queen Darien Quinn and now, all-the-better-to-bite-you-with Chad Albright, she thinks are wonderful and yet she treats Daniel like he's a complete psycho freak womaniser.

Seema says it's good that we all like different types, which I suppose is true, but, as I was kneeling between a silver igloo tent and an enormous fibreglass climbing wall, I wished, just for once, that

Magenta's type would be someone who was worth getting cramp for.

'Ssssh!' Magenta whispered and flapped her hand so that we'd crouch down even further. 'I think I can see him.'

'Madge, you've thought you've seen him about six times since we got here,' Seema pointed out. 'I'm getting bored. I thought we'd come to help you buy your stuff for camping, not embark on personal surveillance.'

'I'm sure this is illegal,' I added.

'I just want to make sure he's here and then we'll come out and just happen to be buying my stuff, so it looks like a complete coincidence.'

'And then what?' Seema persisted.

'Then we'll get talking and – who knows where it might lead.' She turned round to face us. 'Did I tell you his middle name's Indiana?'

'Yes, about twenty times.' Seema was starting to sound tetchy. 'Look, why don't we just buy your stuff and then mooch about for a while and see if Chad turns up? If he doesn't, then just accept that it wasn't meant to be.'

The silver igloo tent was on a raised display podium and Magenta had been peering round the side of it, into the main area of the shop. She turned round to face Seema, looking totally confused, as though Seema had just told her that the Earth was triangular and would end by Christmas. 'What do you mean, accept that it wasn't meant to be? Let's have a little less negativity, please.'

'It's not negativity – it's reality.' Seema shuffled forward so that she was right alongside Madge. 'You know the saying, less is more?' Magenta nodded. 'Well, I think that sometimes you try a bit too hard.' Ooo! Rather Seema than me. 'I just think that if you were just a bit more laid back, then you might have more success with boys.'

Magenta slumped down with her back to a display stand. 'I have lots of success with boys. Look how many boys I've been out with since we've been in Year 9.' Which was exactly Seema's point, but she didn't seem to have got it. Magenta was looking really sad and she started to twiddle with one of the guy ropes from the silver igloo tent. 'So, what are you saying?'

'Nothing,' Seema went on. 'It's just that if it's meant to happen between you and Chad, it'll happen. Just don't force it.'

Magenta was pulling at the end of the guy rope and fraying it out into a fluffy tassel. 'I'm not forcing it. He chose me on stage . . .' She looked at me and added pointedly, '. . . when it was FOR CHARITY.' Then she returned to unravelling the tent cord. 'So he must like me. What's wrong with giving him the chance to choose me again?'

Seema was being so patient. 'Nothing at all. Just don't make yourself quite so available. Play hard to get. Be seductive.'

Magenta seemed to be mulling over Seema's advice. 'Hard to get. Seductive.' She looked up and smiled. 'I can do seductive.'

But then I had a terrible thought. 'What happens if Spud turns up as well? Didn't he say he was coming with Chad to buy his kit?'

Magenta flapped her hand like it was the most ridiculous suggestion in the world. 'Neh! Can you honestly see someone as cool as Chad going shopping with someone like Spud? Never going to happen, Arl.'

'Jeez, if it isn't the weird sisters cooking up a stew.' An American accent boomed out over the top of the taped music in the shop.

Followed by Spud's unmistakable tones. 'Hi, Magenta!'

Chad Albright and Spud had sneaked up and taken us all by complete surprise. I jumped about a metre in the air and Magenta slapped her hand to her chest as though she was having a heart attack. Honestly, she's so dramatic; I don't know why the Drama department don't rate her acting.

'For heaven's sake,' she gasped. 'You scared the life out of me!'

'I thought you said the reason you couldn't go out with me this afternoon was because you were having a fitting for your bridesmaid's dress.' Spud sounded really peed off.

'I am . . . I mean, I was,' Magenta said, quickly. 'Only it's been put off till tonight.'

But before Spud could question her any more, something really creepy happened – this strange hissing sound started and it seemed as if it was coming from somewhere in Magenta's vicinity, like she'd sprung a leak or something.

'What?' She looked from one of us to the other. 'It's not me!' She turned to Chad. 'So . . .' she began but, just at that moment, an orange life-jacket that had been on the display platform wobbled backwards and forwards and toppled over, landing at Madge's feet. 'Oh good grief! Am I in for any more surprises this afternoon?' she said, kicking it away.

'So, anyway, Chad . . .' Madge continued, trying to sound nonchalant, '. . . fancy bumping into you here.'

I was beginning to feel distinctly uneasy because

the hissing was getting louder. Seema and I were looking round to try and find where it was coming from, when a large rucksack that had been propped up on the display stand also began rocking about and then it fell to the floor next to the life-jacket.

'You don't think there's a gas leak, do you?' I asked, starting to get really freaked out.

'What do you mean, fancy bumping into me?' Chad jeered, completely ignoring my extremely rational suggestion and, with it, the possible need to evacuate the building – urgently. 'You were there when we planned this trip, so don't try and pretend it's some spooky coincidence.'

If I hadn't been so concerned about the hissing, I might have had some sympathy for Magenta because it looked like her Plan A had just foundered at first base. I didn't know what her Plan B was, in fact I wasn't even sure she had a Plan B, but, to be honest, right at that moment, I couldn't have cared less. I was more concerned with everyone's safety – mine in particular. If I was injured in some freak gas explosion my parents couldn't help but find out that I'd been out with Madge and then, even if the gas leak didn't kill me, they would.

I was just trying to think up some plausible excuse as to why Magenta and I should just happen to have found ourselves in the same department store at the same time (I'd been threatened with grounding for the duration of my natural life if I went out with her again) when, suddenly, an enormous brass compass rolled off the stand and away across the shop floor. Then the carefully constructed tower of camping cutlery that had been built next to the silver igloo tent tumbled down in a cascade of aluminium. Knives and forks and spoons and can-openers were crashing down and making a terrible din – it was worse than that time when one of the dinner ladies at school slipped on a squashed chip and knocked all the serving tins on the floor.

'What on Earth is wrong with this place?' Magenta said, as a cagoule in Day-Glo lime green took to the air and flopped down on the head of an elderly customer in khaki shorts and Jesus sandals. 'Has there been an earthquake that no one's told us about?'

'Probably a poltergeist,' Spud said, ducking to avoid a low-flying first-aid box.

I was looking round, desperate to find some logical reason why the whole shop seemed to have taken to the air, when I noticed a bright yellow plastic tab on the floor where the life-jacket had fallen. But when I picked it up – eeek! I couldn't believe it. I grabbed

Madge's arm and shook it to try and draw her attention away from Chad Albright.

'What?' She sounded a tad impatient.

'Oh my God, Magenta!' I held out the tab. 'It says, "Pull to inflate". No wonder it's hissing – you've inflated the life-jacket.'

Magenta rolled her eyes, reached over and grabbed the life-jacket. 'Durr!' she said. 'In case it's escaped your notice, it's already inflated and the tab's still on there.'

Then the full horror of what had happened suddenly dawned on us. The cord Magenta had been playing with earlier hadn't been one of the guy ropes from the tent; it had been the rip-cord from an inflatable dinghy that had been folded up on the podium next to us. And worse still, it had had various items of equipment stacked on top of it. When Magenta had jumped up, she must have accidentally pulled the cord and the rubber boat was unfurling like some grotesque yellow marshmallow – in the middle of the shop, flinging enamel plates and cups all over the place.

'Run for it!' Madge said.

Too late! A shop assistant had seen us and was coming towards us, blocking our escape route to the main shop. Just then, a mannequin dressed in a ski jacket, bobble hat and backpack keeled over and hit the man in the Jesus sandals who was fumbling about trying to pull the Day-Glo cagoule off his head. He went head first into a four-man frame tent that had been the central tableau of the department. And still the dinghy was getting bigger and bigger. Torches and camping stoves, water bottles and sleeping bags were being tossed all over the shop and customers were running in every direction, covering their heads and screaming. It was a total nightmare.

'I am dead meat if my parents ever find out about this,' I snapped at Magenta.

'Honestly, Arl,' Madge replied. 'You are unreal sometimes. Can't you think about anyone but yourself?'

Which I thought was a bit much, coming from Magenta. 'OK – let me put it a different way – *you'll* be dead meat, if my parents ever find out about this.'

Just then a set of folding saucepans was catapulted into the air, hitting the shop assistant right on the bridge of his nose. He groaned and stumbled backwards with the impact. I felt terrible, because I knew it must have hurt him something rotten, but also, I couldn't help feeling relieved that it gave us time to make our exit.

'Oi!' he shouted, grabbing a pair of hiking socks

and holding them to his nose – which was gushing blood everywhere. 'Stop them!'

Seema pulled my arm and whispered, 'This way, quick.'

And she ducked round the back of the climbing wall into this gap that was filled with wooden struts and cobwebs. We all followed, even Chad and Spud, and we came out right next to the escalators. Seema's so brilliant.

'Run!' Magenta shouted. Only – typical Madge – instead of running round the other side to the 'down' escalator, she ran straight down the 'up' one. Masses of people were coming up towards us and they weren't at all happy as we pushed our way down one floor after another.

I couldn't believe that we actually got out of the place without being caught but once we were well clear, we stopped to get our breath.

'Ohmigod, Madge!' Seema panted. 'I said be seductive, not destructive.'

Unfortunately Spud seemed to get the wrong end of the stick. 'Oh wow! Were you trying to seduce me, Magenta? That's so sweet.'

Madge screwed her eyes up and gave Seema one of those looks that says, *Now look what you've gone and done.*

Then Chad gave this sneery laugh. 'Man, if that's your idea of seduction, I'd hate to see how you try to put people off you. But I'll say one thing, Magenta – life's never dull when you're around. I can't wait till we go to camp.'

After we'd said goodbye to the boys, we were in Up Front, this really cool shop where Magenta was spending the money her dad had given her for walking boots on this gorgeous dress. She looked really pleased with herself.

'Did you hear Chad? He said he couldn't wait till camp because I'll be there to make it more interesting. I can't wait.'

There's no answer to that, is there? But at least now she's looking forward to camp!

7
Magenta

Didn't I tell you my plan would work? My life is sooo looking up at the moment. There are about a million things for me to look forward to.

The first thing to be excited about is going to camp because:

a) Chad will be there and he said he was looking forward to seeing me. (I knew he wouldn't be able to hold out for long.) And Seema says I don't know how to be seductive! Huh! What does she know?

b) Mr Snowdon is the most gorgeous teacher in the entire school and he's going to be one of the boys' chaperones. You should've seen him climbing the ropes in the gym when someone knocked a shuttlecock into the light fitting – talk about fit! I can't wait to see him abseiling down a rock face!

c) Like Arlette and Seema said, it'll be like a week-long sleepover and we can have midnight feasts and talk about everything all night. Oooo! It'll be brilliant.

d) There are a few good things about being in the country, like sunbathing on the grass and paddling in lakes and . . . well, I'm sure I'll be able to think of some more soon.

e) It means no school for an entire week! Of course, a teensy bit of a downer is that my two worst teachers, Mrs Blobby and The Rhino, are coming with us but at least in the countryside there'll be plenty of trees to hide behind, so I should be able to escape their Gestapo-like gaze without too much of a problem.

Number two in my excitement calendar is that my birthday's coming up soon (OK, so it's not for a couple of months but I'm a big believer in forward planning). And that means:

a) I'll be fourteen like everyone else in my year. Which, actually, is the worst thing about having a birthday at the end of the summer term – from about February onwards everybody's always saying things like, 'Ooo, are you still only thirteen?' like I'm some sort of freak of nature. Honestly, my parents were so unfair having me in the summer. It's not like I'm any less mature than the others in my year but sometimes, the way they go on about my age, you'd think they were older than me or something.

b) My dad won't be able to treat me like a baby any more and tell me I have to be home by nine o'clock.

c) I'll get loads of presents!

And the third really brilliant thing looming on my horizon of truly fab events is my dad's wedding because:

a) I'm going to be the bridesmaid. I've already designed my outfit and chosen this seriously gorgeous dark pink sari fabric with gold embroidery round it. And the dress I've designed has layers of it draped over each other so that I'll look like a princess. Not your average traditional princess, mind you – more a radically cool one.

b) Belinda is really brilliant and when she was my Art teacher, she had a bit of a soft spot for me, which means that if I talk to her nicely, she'll be able to win Dad over and I'll be able to get my own way more often. Because, between you and me, my dad's ideas on parenting date back to medieval times. I think he still secretly believes that kids should be seen and not heard and it's only thanks to Gran's influence that I have any sort of a social life at all.

c) My mum died when I was three, so I don't

really remember her that much and I think it'll be really cool to have a stepmum. We can go shopping together and have serious, in-depth mother/daughter talks about relationships and do lots of female bonding late at night and stuff like you see on TV.

Anyway, Mrs Hemmings, the textile teacher from school, is coming round in a minute. She's helping Belinda make her wedding gown and my bridesmaid's dress so I'm just getting ready to go down and show them my design. I'm having a slight crisis about how to accessorise though – I really need to get my head round it, because with the gold embroidery, I think gold jewellery would work best, but I tend to be more of a silvery sort of person. And of course I'll need to co-ordinate with Belinda because, whatever I decide, she's going to have to do the same otherwise it'll be too clashing. Ooo! I bet Belinda will look beautiful – like a fairytale bride – and, of course, I'll be right there next to her. I can't wait!

'Green!' I couldn't believe my eyes! Belinda and Mrs Hemmings had swatches of fabric spread out all over the floor like some hideous drab-fest patchwork carpet – and there wasn't one that even remotely resembled the amazing sari fabric I'd picked out. This lot looked more like Iron-Age rags that had been used to clean out the cowshed. 'You never said anything about green! Bridesmaids are supposed to look pretty.'

Belinda was sitting cross-legged on the floor doing her 'peace and love' act. 'You will look pretty, Magenta, trust me.' Trust her? I'd rather trust Sweeney Todd with a carving knife! 'Your dad and I did tell you that we wanted our wedding to be environmentally friendly.'

'Never mind the environment; what about me?' I was in a state of shock. 'There's nothing friendly about expecting me to wear that! In fact, if you ask me, it amounts to bridesmaid-abuse!'

'You know we're very keen to make sure everything comes from sustainable and organic sources,' she went on. Which in normal, non-eco-speak means I'm going to be wearing a mouldy dish-cloth and eating recycled hamster food!

Mrs Hemmings was examining her feet and trying to pretend she wasn't there when Gran poked her head round the door. Gran and her sister, Auntie Venice, are a couple of geriatric Hell's Angels and Gran was wearing her leathers, obviously having just come back from a burn-up with Auntie Vee, on their motorbike.

'Everything all right in here? Anyone fancy a cup of tea? Camomile for you, Belinda, love?' My gran always talks in one long sentence and hardly even pauses for breath.

'No everything is *not* all right! Did you know about this?' I challenged.

Gran screwed up her eyes and stared at me as though I'd just been speaking Ancient Chinese. 'I'm afraid you've lost me there, Magenta love. Know about what?'

I picked up one of the pieces of material and flapped it in Gran's face. 'That my big day is going to be ruined because I'm expected to wear a tie-dye T-shirt dress the colour of snot?'

Belinda took a deep breath and turned to Mrs Hemmings. 'Ann, would you mind giving Florence a hand making the tea? There's some carrot cake in the cupboard too, so help yourself.' Then, when they'd gone she turned back to me. 'Why don't you sit down and let's talk about this, Magenta. I really think you're overreacting.'

'Overreacting?' The cheek of the woman! 'Actually, Belinda, I think my reaction is perfectly normal considering that I've just been told I'm going to walk down the aisle wearing something that looks like a used hankie!'

And then she dropped the neutron bomb. Sorry, correction – the *first* neutron bomb. 'Well, that's the other thing I wanted to talk to you about – there won't be an aisle as such. Your dad and I have chosen to have an Earth ceremony.'

An Earth ceremony? Did I say Belinda was cool? Well, rewind. The woman is obviously a complete headcase. Who in their right mind has an Earth ceremony apart from hippies and total drongos? And, as for my dad – has he finally flipped? Well, actually, that's always been a matter for debate but we won't go into that here.

'What do you mean, an Earth ceremony?' I asked, trying very hard to keep my voice a couple of octaves below the level that would shatter glass.

'Well, we've found a pastor who's willing to preside over a commitment ceremony in the woods behind the reservoir . . .'

'In the woods!' Second neutron bomb! 'So it's not enough that you're sending me into the wilderness for a week with the school to catch pneumonia, you expect me to come home and get double pneumonia standing knee deep in mud, watching you and my dad going all gooey-eyed over each other in some forest ritual, wearing a dress that'll probably look as though Sirius has dragged it round the garden about a billion times!'

'It won't be like that,' she said, trying to be all reasonable. 'We're looking for an alternative venue for if it rains and you won't get cold because the dresses I've designed for you and Justine . . .'

Whoa! Did she say Justine? Third bombshell. If you're not up to scratch with my life, Justine is my double-crossing, loud-mouthed, spoilt-brat cousin from hell – and, just in case you're in any doubt – we don't get on.

'I thought *I* was going to be your bridesmaid.' My voice was rapidly rising up the scale towards panic pitch.

'I prefer the term attendant rather than bridesmaid . . .' Wooooooo! Ex! Cuse! Me! '. . . but yes all three of you are going to be my attendants.'

'Three?' Gran's crystal vase was in serious danger by this point because I was really struggling to control my vocal cords.

'Didn't your dad tell you?' Belinda went on. 'I'm having you, Justine and Holden.'

And that was when my world finally went into nuclear meltdown! Holden is Justine's grub of a brother and he takes irritation to new depths. There was no way I was walking down the aisle or the forest glade or anywhere (except possibly through the gates of Hell) with that little gnat-weasel.

'You know what, Belinda! You can keep your stupid Earth ceremony – and your stupid camouflage creations. I'm not even going to go to the wedding. End of!'

I headed for the door but Belinda called me back. 'Wait a minute, Magenta, please. Just have a look at the designs, I'm sure they're not as bad as you think.'

'What's the point?' I shouted. 'Why don't you just stick everyone in bin bags and have done with it? Oh – sorry, I forgot – they're not biodegradable!'

And I walked out – making sure I slammed the door very loudly, so that she knew how much she'd upset me. Then I slammed my bedroom door too – just for good measure.

Honestly, life is so unfair! And Belinda didn't even seem remotely sorry for totally ruining my dream wedding! Did I say I was looking forward to Dad marrying her? Well forget it! Cinderella got a better deal than me on the stepmother front.

She might want to ruin my life, but there was no way I was going to let her ruin my Saturday night too. I flopped down on the bed and looked for some moral support. First I texted Arlette but she sent one back saying that she and Seema were going to the pictures with Ben and Hayden. Honestly – I fall over backwards for my friends but they don't have any consideration for me in my hour of need. I even tried Chelsea Riordan but she and Hattie Pringle were going round to the Lyles' house to see Magnus and Angus. People can be so selfish at times. My life had gone from truly brilliant to a miserable black hole of depression in ten minutes and no one seemed to even care. Of course I could've rung Spud, but I hadn't quite reached the any-port-in-a-storm level of self-pity yet.

I couldn't even watch television because I'm not allowed one in my room. Dad reckons it spoils family life – yeah right! And marrying the control-freak from Hippy-ville doesn't?

And just to make matters ten gazillion times worse, I could hear Daniel's TV through the wall from his room next door. Normally when my life is in ruins I can go over the balcony and talk to him, but that particular route back to sanity was also closed to me. He was still doing this big macho thing round school, ignoring me at every opportunity. He is so pathetic. I don't know what I ever saw in him anyway. I mean, don't get me wrong, Daniel was great as a mate but, as boyfriends go, it was never going to work. He's way too immature for me. I mean, any reasonable person would have been able to listen to my explanation but not Daniel – oh no! He has to make a bi-ig drama out of it and then he's insensitive enough to flaunt Miz Muscle right under my nose! You see what I mean about it not mattering that I have a summer birthday? Daniel was fourteen back in September – nearly a year older than me – and look at how he's behaved.

I have to admit, I was just starting to feel a teensy bit sorry for myself (and even contemplated phoning Spud!) when there was a knock on my door.

'Magenta, love, can I have a word?' It was Gran. 'Only, your dad's come home and when Belinda told him what had happened . . .' The traitor! '. . . he wasn't very happy.' So what's new? My dad suffers from terminal stroppiness, in fact he's a prime candidate for Rageoholics Anonymous, so how Gran thought that this insignificant piece of non-news was supposed to make me open my door, I don't know! '. . . so I thought it might be a good idea for us to have a little chat before you went downstairs.'

I was just about to tell her that on the scale of one to ten of good ideas, hers was well into the minus figures, when a thought struck me; if I showed Gran my design, she'd see how gorgeous it was and she'd have a word with Dad and Belinda. When they saw how much better my dress was than the one Belinda had designed, they'd change their minds about having a stupid Earth ceremony and maybe even let me design Belinda's dress too!

I was just about to unlock the door to Gran when there was a tap on my French windows and Daniel was standing there. I don't know how long he'd been there because it was drizzling outside and his hair was so wet it'd all stuck to his head. Actually, he looked quite cute.

'Are you OK?' he mouthed through the glass.

'Magenta, love, open the door,' Gran persisted. 'Belinda's terribly upset.' Hmph! She should've thought of that before she tried to dress me like the mud fairy – but, on the other hand, I did want to get my point across. What a dilemma!

'Magenta!' Ooops! That was Dad and he sounded about as friendly as a velociraptor with a migraine. 'Come out immediately!'

Suddenly there was no dilemma – I opened the French windows and slipped out on to the balcony.

'Ssssh!' I whispered to Daniel, pushing him back towards his own room.

Once we were well out of the way I closed Daniel's French windows and sat down on his bed. I could

97

still hear Dad hammering on my door through the wall but I was well out of his reach, so I ignored it.

'This doesn't mean anything, you know,' I said quickly, just in case Daniel thought I'd forgiven him for going off with Kara Kennedy.

He shrugged. 'I heard your door slam so I wondered if you were all right – that's all.'

Which, actually, was quite sweet of him. And, as I said, Daniel used to be brilliant as a friend – it was just when you stuck 'boy' at the beginning that the problems started, so maybe we could just get back to being mates again?

'How come you're not out with Kara tonight?' I asked – and it hardly hurt at all, saying her name.

'Oh, she's got an athletics meet somewhere,' he said. 'How about you? Why aren't you out with Spud?'

'Erm?' What could I say? So I changed the subject. 'Do you fancy going out to The Filling Station for a coffee or something?'

Stroke of genius, or what? Talk about killing two birds with one brainwave! Not only did it mean Daniel and I could get back on track, but it also meant that if we were quick, we could sneak downstairs and out of Daniel's door before Dad had even realised I'd gone. I don't want to be conceited or anything, but sometimes I amaze even myself.

So there we were, sitting in The Filling Station over a slice of pizza and a Coke. I told Daniel all about the hideous Glasto-chick bridesmaid outfit I'm expected to wear and he was smiling as I was describing it. He really is a brilliant mate – I don't know why we risked our friendship for the sake of a few snogs. And then I started to tell him about this afternoon in Farrago and he laughed, but in a nice way, which was really sweet of him.

Suddenly, he looked across the table and started to bite his lip, which is usually a sign that he's going to morph into his serious mode – and that freaks me out, to be honest.

'I have really missed you, you know, Magenta.' He went all pink and looked down at the table, which is so cute – he's been doing that since he was about six. 'Do you think there's any chance we could forget the last couple of weeks and go back to how we were?'

Phew! I'd thought things were going to get heavy for a minute – what a relief!

'Course!' I said, picking an olive off my pizza and putting it on Daniel's plate. 'In fact, to be honest, I've really missed talking to you too.'

So, there we are! Daniel and I are mates again. I mean, how mature are we? Some people let arguments drag on for months, or even years, but not us. Of course he has his moods – in fact he seems a bit tetchy again now – but, as a true friend, I just need to accept that Daniel is going through some hormone changes, which is quite normal for boys – old Jones the Bones told us that in PSE.

I've just ordered us another couple of Cokes with what's left of the money Dad gave me to buy my camping kit, so I'm sure he'll cheer up again soon. I'm just happy we're all sorted in time to go to camp. It'll be so brilliant to be able to go round there and talk to him about it. I can't wait.

8
Daniel

I've come to the decision that life's like a massive game of snakes and ladders; just when you think you're chugging along nicely, getting sorted and hurtling along the top row with square one hundred within your sights – bosh! This dirty great serpent rears its ugly head and you have to go back to the beginning – without passing Go, without collecting two hundred pounds and not a ladder in sight.

A few weeks ago, I was going out with the girl of my dreams, I had a great gang of mates, a nice home with a pretty cool mum (OK, Joe was a bit of a pain in the butt, but you can't have everything), I saw my dad regularly and I had a dream of becoming a top DJ. That magic square at the top of the board was beckoning. But now look at me – my life sucks!

You're probably thinking that this is all about Magenta (again!) but this time you're wrong. In fact, the last knock-back from Magenta really put things in perspective for me. When we went to The Filling Station, I laid my heart on the table. I told her how much I'd missed her and everything, but she made it crystal clear that she just wanted to be friends.

What could I say? I remember Mum saying to me, 'The first golden rule of relationships, Daniel – you can't go out with someone who doesn't want to go out with you.' I think that was at the Year 6 Christmas party. Magenta was standing under the mistletoe and I really wanted to kiss her but she blew a raspberry at me and everyone laughed. You see, three and a half years on and she's still blowing raspberries at me! So, that's it – I'm not taking it any more. I have well and truly banished all thoughts of Magenta as a possible girlfriend from my head and, after all, I'd rather be friends with her than not even on speaking terms. Any romantic interest I had in her is over, ended, finished, finito!

No, Magenta was nothing at all to do with the anaconda that rose up from the bowels of my life and ambushed me; it came from a totally unexpected (and previously supportive) quarter, which is why it's really doing my head in.

But I'm getting ahead of myself. Let me go back to before half term when I had my careers interview and the downward spiral really started.

It was already all round school that lamebrain Angus Lyle had told the careers bloke that his main interest was fires, and the dipstick only went and suggested he looked at a career in the fire service. So you can imagine the level of confidence I had in the guy before I even went in. Although, to be fair, it seems that Angus forgot to mention that he preferred lighting fires to putting them out!

But, even apart from that, by the time it came to my appointment, I was hardly in the right frame of mind to decide the course of my entire life. What with all the emotional strain I'd been under recently with my broken leg *and* my broken heart, not to mention a girlfriend who sees more of her tracksuit than she does of me, when I walked through the door of the careers office, my future was already looking cloudier than a fog-load of cumulus. In fact, I was so fed up, that the idea of becoming a DJ had gone right out of the window and I'd narrowed down my job choices to anything that had minimal contact with other human beings – and girls in particular. Which left me with:

1) astronaut
2) Siberian salt miner
3) snow-ologist stationed at the South Pole, or
4) monk
(With the Foreign Legion thrown in as a possible optional extra)

'All good,' Magnus agreed when I showed him my

list as we were sitting at the back in Geography, beforehand. 'But I'm thinking Siberia and the South Pole are seriously cold places to spend the rest of your life.'

He had a point. Winter's never been my favourite season, my nose always goes bright pink and my brother calls me Rudolph, so, in the interest of my self-confidence, I thought I'd better cross those two off.

Magnus looked down my list again and shook his head. 'A monk? Seriously?'

'What's wrong with being a monk?' Which was a fair question, I thought. After all, they do a good job, they don't have bills to pay and they've got plenty of food – although I think it's probably a bit top-heavy on the home-grown fruit and veg and lacking on the chips and pizza front. But I can just see myself mooching round the cloisters with my hood up, looking all mean and moody. Plus – added bonus points – not a girl in sight!

'I have one word to say on that score, Danno – footwear!'

Again – a good point. It was bad enough when my leg was in plaster – my toes felt like frozen chipolatas most of the time – so the thought of schlepping around in open-toed sandals all year round was a bit of a turn-off.

'And,' he added, 'just a thought, but I'm thinking monks need to be religious. Possibly?'

OK, so that was three of my job prospects crossed off, which left me with astronaut and Foreign Legion.

'You know, they do have some girls in space now, so you might want to rethink the whole astronaut thing too.' I was beginning to regret showing Magnus my list.

'Yes,' I said, 'but think of the zero gravity training. That would be well cool.'

'True!' he conceded.

But then I remembered that I got airsick when we went to Spain the year before last, which might be a slight problem in terms of space flight. So, by the time my fifteen minutes with the careers guy came round, my job prospects had been reduced to joining the Foreign Legion. The only problem there was that his computer wouldn't accept it as a valid career choice and, after he'd punched in all my details and interests, it came up with the totally rancid idea that I should go into teaching. Yeah right! Like I'm going to stand up in front of people like my brother and let them make mincemeat out of me. It might as well have suggested that I aim for a career with the Kamikaze aerobatics team!

I spent the rest of the week studying all the male

teachers in our school and trying to find one that rated above two and a half on my role model scale of one to ten. The only one who even approached the cool rating was Mr Snowdon, the PE teacher, and that's because he used to play semi-pro football and once got into the third round of the FA cup and also, at the school disco last year, he did some mean body-popping when it was my set. I looked at the rest of them with their tweed jackets and short-back-and-sides haircuts. Was that really going to be my future? To stand at the front of a class like a total nerd with gross nasal hair twisting out of my nostrils and Biro ink all over a checked shirt, while a group of morons chucked chewed-up paper balls at me! My life was well and truly over.

Even the half-term holiday was a bit of a write-off. I hardly saw anyone for the entire week because:

1) Curtis insisted that Magenta had to go in to work with him every day of the holiday to pay back the money she spent on clothes instead of her kit for camp. (But, actually, she showed me the dress she bought and she did look really cute in it. And the silvery bits in it made her eyes look extra sparkly and gorgeous – purely in a friends sort of way, you understand.)

2) Kara was on a tennis course at some big-name

sports centre. I think I was supposed to be impressed but she might as well have said she was going clog dancing in the Klondike, for all it meant to me. I did phone her a couple of times but she didn't even ask how I was or what I'd been doing! She was all, 'I've got the fastest serve of any girl here,' and 'I'm even faster than some of the boys at sprinting,' and 'The coach says my forehand volley's even stronger than Steffi Graf's was at my age.' So I was feeling well pissed off with her.

3) Even though Spud and I are speaking again, he's been keeping his distance. And I don't need to be the reincarnation of Sigmund Freud to know what that's all about. He's reached warp factor ten on the guilty conscience scale about going out with Magenta and, to be honest, it's about time! So I'm going to let him stew.

4) Magnus and Angus went to their grandparents at Hastings for half term.

So it was me, the PS2 and my vision of myself in twenty years' time – wearing grey flannel trousers and brown brogues and being on my own because no one wanted to know me – for the entire week.

By the time the end of the holiday came, I was

heading for a major Prozac alert! We go back to school tomorrow and of course I was looking forward to the school camping trip that's happening next week. In fact, this morning, Magenta was in and out of my room just like the old days, which cheered me up a bit.

'OK, Daniel, which one shall I take?' She was standing on the balcony in front of my French windows with one T-shirt tucked under her chin and two others on hangers, one in each hand. 'Do you think the pink one, or the one with the smiley face, or the one with the glittery bits?' But before I could answer, she shrugged her shoulders. 'Never mind, I'd better take all three just to be on the safe side.'

A couple of minutes later she was back. 'Now – shoes?' She looked so sweet standing there with four left shoes tucked under her arms. 'Do you think there'll be any call to wear these?' She held out a pair of flip-flops with glitter and flowers all over them. 'I know they're a bit flimsy, but I'm thinking they might be quite nice to wear round the campfire in the evening. And, I could paint my nails the same colour as the flowers.'

'Didn't they give you a kit list?' I asked. I was so pleased we were getting on again.

She flapped her hand dismissively. 'Yes, but that's just plain stupid. I mean, how can anyone be expected to take only one suitcase for a whole week?'

'Easily,' I replied. I'd already packed my stuff (I'd had nothing else to do all week) and it was crammed into a backpack that Mum had used in her student days. 'I really don't think we'll need very much.'

'Speak for yourself, Daniel, but I have no intention of smelling like a farmyard for seven days. Now, just run through this checklist with me, will you?'

She sat down on my bed next to me and, I must admit, I did get the beginnings of a flutter in my tummy but I made very sure I stopped myself even going there. Magenta and I are friends and that's how it's going to stay. So, I stood up and went over to the desk where my computer is.

'Go on, hit me with it,' I said, not being remotely prepared for what was coming.

'OK – I'm going to start at the top and work down,' she said in a very businesslike way. 'Shampoo, conditioner, mousse, hair drier, hair glitter, hair spray, hair curling wand, hair straightener, hair crimper . . .' She was taking more hair products than Boots. In fact she probably needed a cabin trunk just for her head.

'Whoa!' I interrupted. 'Why do you need hair curlers *and* hair straighteners?'

'Because I just do,' she said. 'Anyway, you're not a girl and you just wouldn't understand.'

Fair point. 'OK, but can I ask one question?'

Magenta sighed. 'What?'

'These curlers and straighteners, how do they work?'

'What do you mean, how do they work? They heat up and then one curls your hair and one straightens it, depending on your mood – and the occasion, of course.'

'Are they battery operated, or solar?'

She rolled her eyes. 'No, silly – you have to plug them in.'

'Plug them into . . .?' I waited.

'Durr – a plug socket.'

I nodded, hoping the penny would drop soon, but Magenta was looking at me with her eyes screwed up and her head on one side, as though she was trying to work out some incredibly difficult mathematical equation. She looked really cute, actually.

It was clear I was going to have to spell it out. 'OK, how many tents have you seen with sockets?'

Suddenly she looked shocked. 'Tents?'

'Yes, tents – as in camping.'

'But Arlette said when she went camping with the church they were in wooden huts on bunk beds!'

Oh, poor Magenta. She was genuinely shaken by the revelation that we were going to be sleeping under canvas.

'Haven't you spoken to any of the Year 10s who went last year?' I asked.

'Yeah, right! Like that's going to be my first choice topic of conversation.'

I took my kit list down from my notice-board and went and sat down next to her. 'You've got a sleeping bag, right?'

She nodded. 'But I thought that was just for a bit of added warmth in case there weren't enough blankets on the bunk beds.'

'What about your bed roll? Didn't that give you any clues that we'd be sleeping on the ground?'

'On the ground!'

'What did you think it meant?'

She shrugged. 'I thought the secretary had made a typing mistake and it was talking about a packed lunch.' I was aching to put my arm round her and comfort her but I wasn't sure whether that might be overstretching our 'friends' status. 'They can't possibly expect us to sleep on the ground. There might be creepy-crawlies and everything.'

But just at that point, Mum called me down for lunch.

'Look, I've got to go now but I'll come round later and we can talk about it some more. Don't worry about anything – you'll be OK.'

But, due to the enormous venomous snake that was about to rear up and devour me, it didn't quite work out that way.

At this point you need to know that my mum has this big thing about us having Sunday lunch together on the weekends that Joe and I don't go to Dad's. She thinks it brings us closer as a family – which, if she really looked at the relationship between her two sons, she'd see is clearly not working. But anyway, it's a pretty big thing for her to have the three of us sitting round the table every other week – so you can imagine my surprise when I went down and there were four places set.

'Huh! Who else is coming?' I asked.

'A friend of mine,' she said, looking a bit sheepish. 'Now give me a hand carrying things through from the kitchen, please, and give your brother a shout.'

A friend? How come she was allowed to invite a friend round to the sacred Sunday lunch ritual but whenever I'd asked if Magenta could come it was, 'Oh no, this is for *family*!'

I shouted for Joe, but I'd have needed a megaphone to penetrate the thousand decibels of rap that was pumping out from his room.

'So who is this friend?' I asked as I took the tureen of potatoes through to the dining room.

'Erm . . .' Mum was straightening the tablecloth like her life depended on it. 'It's Donald,' she said in this ultra-normal voice. 'You remember – you met him at the hospital bazaar at Christmas.'

Donald! Not the Donald she'd introduced me to who was running the tombola stall and was about a hundred and ten – well, sixty anyway – who was wearing a hand-knitted cardigan and had his glasses on a chain? But before I could ask, the doorbell rang and there was Donald – only this time he had a *machine*-knitted cardigan on and his glasses were on top of his head. And instead of the tombola, he had a bunch of flowers in his hand. But then as he came in he kissed Mum, which is pretty normal, you might think, except that he kissed her on the lips. Eeek!

'Hello, Daniel,' he said in a strong Scottish accent, putting out his hand to shake mine. 'Good to meet you again.'

'Er, cheers!' I shook his hand and then ran upstairs to take refuge in Joe's room.

'Wazzup?' Joe said as I burst through his door then

113

slammed it shut and stood with my back pressed against it.

'Mum's got a boyfriend! And he's ancient!' I burst out, expecting Joe to look as shocked as I was.

'Yeah, I know. The old Scottish geezer.' He turned the volume down on his stereo so that I didn't have to lip-read.

'You know?' I couldn't believe it.

'Yeah, been going on for ages.'

'Ages! How long is ages? Months? Years?'

'Just a few months,' he said, like it was nothing.

'And how d'you find out about it?'

'Whoa! Way too much information required here. It's gonna cost ya, little bro.'

And that was it. All my *no-more-Mr-Nice-guy* training came into effect. I sprang across the room, grabbed Joe by the throat and pushed him against the wall.

'Speak or die!' I threatened as Joe scrabbled about on his bed, trying to get away from me. But I had him tight. Wow – all that time on crutches had really paid off. My arm muscles were so pumped up even Arnie would've found it hard to break away. 'I'm warning you – this is not a joke. Tell me everything you know – now!'

'Easy, tiger,' Joe said. 'Just back off, will you?' I

released my grip and Joe rubbed his neck. 'Jeez! Who rattled your cage?'

'Just tell me everything.'

It turns out that Donald is an administrator at the hospital and Mum's been going out with him since Christmas! (I'd noticed she'd started wearing make-up to work a while back but I thought she just wanted to cheer up the patients.) Anyway, one Saturday just before Easter when Joe was working in the minimart, he saw them in a car together and they were kissing – eewwww! And to make matters worse, my treacherous mother told Joe to keep it a secret from me. I felt like I was some little kid who couldn't be trusted. I was gutted.

'Boys! Lunch!' the traitor called up from downstairs.

I stared at Joe. I was fuming and I think he knew that I was not to be messed with. 'Is there anything else?'

Joe shrugged. 'Well, only that I think it's serious between them.'

'How serious?'

But I needn't have bothered asking because Mum was only too keen to let us know how serious it was. 'Donald and I have an announcement to make,' she said, staring hard at the tablecloth. 'I know this will probably come as a bit of a shock to you, but we're going to get married.'

Married! This wasn't just serious, this was brain-frying material.

'I know this has come out of the blue . . .' Understatement of the decade! '. . . but it's a bit of a surprise to us too, actually.' She tried to smile but Joe and I just glared at her. She cleared her throat. 'Donald and I have known each other as friends for about five years now, although we've only been going out since Christmas.'

She gave us some rubbish about not telling us until they were sure about each other because she didn't want us to bond with Donald and then be traumatised if it didn't work out (no chance of that). She went on about how I threw a wobbler last time she got herself a boyfriend – a minor detail conveniently omitted was that I was only *ten* at the time! And then she said that she was worried about telling *me* in particular because I've never really taken to any of Dad's girlfriends – which is true, but a limpet on superglue would find it hard to take to some of Dad's girlfriends!

'Why didn't you tell me when Joe found out?' I said, pushing the gravy boat across the table and slopping a big brown splodge of gravy on to her precious tablecloth.

'To be sure, Daniel love, I thought you'd got enough on your plate with your broken leg and Magenta and your SATs. I didn't want to risk upsetting you.' Yeah, right! Well, that worked, didn't it?

'But why d'you have to get married?' I asked. 'Loads of people live together.' The bottom line was, I didn't want a stepdad. We've been getting on fine for years, the three of us – well, two of us got on fine – Joe was a pain in the elbow. I didn't need some geriatric to waltz in and marry my mum. She was happy as she was – wasn't she?

And just when I thought I'd slithered to the end of the snake and was firmly at the bottom of my pit of despair, she put the boot in and sent me crashing even further into the abyss.

'I was coming to that.' She was looking about as comfortable as a snowman in a sauna and, I'm not proud of this, you understand – but I was glad. 'The thing is, Donald's been offered early retirement.' You see! I told you he was old! 'Which means he's leaving the hospital in July and he's always had a dream to buy a salmon farm near Loch Lomond.'

I felt a momentary glimmer of hope, as though

someone had just presented me with an enormous ladder and I could climb back up to sanity. Because, if Donald was moving back to Scotland, then he'd be out of our lives, wouldn't he? Or at least most of the time. I'm sure my mum's sensible enough to handle a long-distance relationship.

Mum cleared her throat. 'So I wanted to talk to you both about how you . . . er . . . felt about us all . . . er . . . moving to Scotland.'

I was numb. If someone had come along with a couple of nine-inch nails and inserted one up each nostril, I don't think I'd have felt a thing. Scotland! She couldn't be serious. It was miles away. Miles away from Magenta, from my friends, from Dad – from everything I'd ever known. I felt like one of those people who's strapped to a giant target with someone throwing knives at me – and that someone was my own mother and her knives were all hitting me – right where it hurts!

Joe was the first to react. He put both hands up and adopted the 'back off' pose. Then he pushed his chair away from the table.

'Leave me out of it. I'm sixteen. I'll just go and live with Dad. Over to you, Danny-boy.' Then he left the room and I heard the front door slam. Cheers, bro. Way to go, sticking together!

I could see Mum had tears in her eyes but I didn't feel at all sorry for her. And then Donald stupid Duck put his hand out and took hold of one her hands.

'The education system in Scotland's excellent,' the slime bag was saying to me.

Education system! Did he seriously think that education was top of my list of priorities at the moment? I stood up, picked up my plate and left the table.

'I'm going to eat this in my room,' I said.

But I didn't eat it. There was a lump the size of a rugby ball in my throat every time I tried. Magenta had been hammering on my French window for ages but I didn't answer. My blind was down and the light off, so she went away in the end and then I heard her at the front door. I don't know what Mum told her, but it's been all quiet from that direction for a while now.

I'm staring up at Sarah Michelle and thinking she's getting a bit tatty round the edges now. I really ought to change her but what's the point if I'm going to be abducted and carted off to the Highlands never to be seen at Archimedes High again? Of course there are a few options that have come to me while I've been lying here:

1) I could join a circus. In Year 7 I did this brilliant apparatus routine using the ropes and the trapeze and I think there's definite potential there that could be developed.

2) I know the careers guy said the Foreign Legion doesn't exist any more, but I'm wondering if there's a junior branch of the SAS?

3) I could run away to my French pen-friend's. Although, I only wrote to him once – his name was Anton or Antoine or something and he lived in Dieppe – or was it Dijon? I know it definitely began with a D, though.

4) Or, if we're following the running away theme, there's always my Auntie Trixie who lives in Ireland. She's two raisins short of a fruitcake and has a cringe factor of about a hundred and ten but she hasn't got any kids of her own and I'm pretty sure she'd give me loads of attention.

5) And I suppose there's always the staying with Dad option, even though my barracuda-brained brother has got in there first. But it's worth a thought.

6) Or, of course, I could go to Scotland with Mum and the duck and be miserable on some remote fish farm and become a teacher and wear a tweed kilt for the rest of my life.

And I'm supposed to be going to camp tomorrow. How can I go away for a week with this hanging over me? And I'm really not up for talking to anyone about it. I just want to get my own head round it before all my so-called mates start putting their oars in. I suppose on the positive side, at least if I go to Scotland Joe wouldn't be there to get up my nose all the time. But then, neither would Magenta.

Oh, this is just *too* harsh!

9

Magenta

OK – ways that the stepmother from hell is systematically ruining my life:

1) I missed out on the whole of my half-term holiday because SHE told Dad that SHE thought it would be a good idea for me to earn back the money I'd spent instead of buying boots for camp. (Didn't I tell you Belinda was turning into something from the Brothers Grimm?) The fact that the dress I bought is so part of my camping equipment in terms of 'round the campfire evening wear', seems way too avant-garde for her farmyard fashion sense.

2) Her chosen method of torture was to send me into work with my dad, which meant:

a) I had to get up at seven o'clock every morning which is even earlier than when I'm at school and,

b) I was a victim of child abuse all week with things like – 'Magenta, do five million photocopies of this,' and 'Magenta, post these nine gazillion letters,' and 'Magenta, file this half a rainforest of paperwork.' I'm only surprised he didn't send me up the chimney!

3) SHE (aka Cruella De Vil) only went out and bought me the most hideous clodhoppers in the history of footwear – without me even trying them on! (Some pathetic excuse about me not being available because I was working – oh, and I wonder whose fault that was in the first place?) I was just trying to get my head round the idea of wearing DMs – which, to be honest, aren't really my scene but you can get some funky flowery ones now which are kind of cool – in an outward-boundy sort of way – when SHE comes home with these totally gross dark brown things, with soles that are about ten centimetres thick and look like tractor tyres. SHE said they were 'proper walking boots'. Yeah right! Like anyone with normal-sized leg muscles could even lift their foot off the ground in those. They're more like something designed to keep deep-sea divers from floating up to the surface. I just hope I don't step in any deep puddles at camp or I might never be seen again – and then she'd be sorry. Or maybe not! Oh my God! What if this is all part of her plan to get me out of her life? I'd phone Dad to warn him except that The Blob

has confiscated everyone's phones for the whole week of camp.

As if it wasn't bad enough that my dad's fiancée is trying to bump me off and I have no communication with the outside world, Daniel is being mean and horrible to me as well – and after he'd said all that stuff about being friends again. I should've known better than to trust someone who goes through girlfriends like most people go through socks.

Take yesterday – I was having major traumas getting everything packed and he promised he'd come round after lunch and help, but did he show up? I don't think so. Then this morning, I was struggling to get my suitcases round to the coach and do you think he came and helped me? Not a sign of him. He wouldn't come to his French window and, even when I knocked at the front door, Mary gave some lame excuse about him not being ready yet – which is so not true because he was only taking one little backpack and that was all sorted yesterday afternoon. I just know he was trying to avoid me but I'd already told Dad and the she-devil that I could manage and I didn't need a lift round to school. Which meant that I had to drag my cases all on my own. (I know the kit list said we were only allowed one small bag but, honestly, I think the person who wrote it must be totally fashion-challenged because there was no way anyone with even the teeniest sense of personal presentation could fit everything for an entire week into one tiny little suitcase.)

I'd borrowed the matching cases on wheels that Dad had bought for his honeymoon, plus, Auntie Venice had lent me a little flight case for the journey essentials, like mascara, face glitter and lip-gloss. The problem was, Dad's cases have got wheels that are more suited to a Dinky toy than a suitcase and as I was pulling them down the road they kept toppling over. First one would keel over and then I'd just get that one straight when the other would go. And I'd balanced Auntie Vee's flight bag on top so that it kept falling off too. Unfortunately, the clasp got all dented as it hit the pavement one time, which was so not my fault – it was because of the stupid Toy Town-sized wheels on Dad's cases, but do you think Auntie Venice is going to see it that way? She's never quite forgiven me for the time when I scrubbed her saucepans till they were nice and shiny – only I didn't know they were supposed to be black because it was a non-stick coating!

Anyway, it took me for ever just to walk round the corner to school. And, by the time I got there, both my heels were grazed where the cases had rolled into them, my wrist was killing me where it got twisted round as the case fell over and I had a bruise the size of a saucer on my calf where Auntie Vee's bag had fallen on to it. Which means that shorts and skirts are now totally out of the question. There's no way I'm going to be revealing my legs looking as though I've just been paint-balling with purple paint. And that is so unfair because my new dress would've looked fabulous when the firelight caught the silvery bits. It would've been all shimmery and gorgeous and Chad would've been blown away.

To make matters worse, when I got round to the school, the Deathwatch Duo: Mrs Blobby and The Rhino, descended on me like a pair of fire-breathing dragons.

'The kit list clearly states one small suitcase or bag, Magenta. You are going to Wales for a week, not the Outer Hebrides for a year,' The Blob ranted. 'Normally when students flout the rules they are sent home and not allowed to go to camp.' Oh yes! 'But I suspect that if I did that I would be playing right into your hands, so I am personally going to supervise you while you empty out your bags.'

Can you believe it? I mean how vindictive is that, to dangle a glimmer of hope in front of me and then snatch it away before going in for the kill with death by total humiliation? And she stood there and watched as I had to repack the whole of my luggage on the pavement – in front of everyone.

Of course then Gran had to come round to take home the other case with all the stuff that The Blob wouldn't let me take and even *she* was up for an Oscar for best supporting role in the I-told-you-so stakes.

And, just to complete my worst nightmare scenario, by the time I got on to the coach I couldn't see any empty places – except for one!

'Yo, Magenta! I've saved you a place.'

Oh great! The only seat left was sitting next to Spud. But even worse, he hadn't even got us places on the back row! And everyone (well, everyone with even a smidgen of credibility, which if you think about it excludes Spud, so I don't know why I should expect any different) knows that the back seat is the coolest place to sit. But had he got us places there – of course not! He'd let that go to such complete deadheads as Angus Lyle, Kara (the cow) Kennedy and Daniel. We were sitting halfway down the coach, which is total social suicide. Something about him getting travel-sick if he sits at the back – great! So, not only am I miles away from my friends but I'm also going to spend the next three hours holding a chuck bucket. Although if he doesn't upgrade his conversational skills, it might be me who needs to throw.

Anyway, we'd been travelling for almost three hours and I was in danger of slipping into a coma I was so bored. My mates were all at the back of the coach and my soon-to-be-dumped boyfriend had been asleep for most of the journey – thank goodness. Being the sort of person who always looks on the positive side, at least with Spud asleep, it meant that I didn't have to discuss the merits of the four four two line-up versus the single striker – yawn, yawn. I seriously question how boys manage to get through life without major brain damage. Although when I looked at Spud with his mouth wide open, his hair flopping across his face and a little drop of dribble trickling down his chin, I concluded that some of them don't. How could I ever have gone out with him in the first place? He was so going to be dumped the minute we got to camp.

I hadn't even had a chance to speak to Seema and Arlette because The Great Pink Blob wouldn't let us out of our seats and she wouldn't even let us stop to get out and stretch our legs or go to the loo.

'No time to stop,' she said, when Hari Gulati said

he needed to go to the toilet. 'Thanks to the selfishness of certain people we are already well behind schedule. And it's only half an hour till we get there.' I hadn't a clue who she was talking about, but if I ever find out, I'll give them a piece of my mind. Some people have no consideration for others. Although, as a teacher you'd think she should know that there are serious health and safety issues around not letting us stop.

I kept turning round and waving to Seema and Arlette and they waved back but I was feeling really lonely, I can tell you. I'd read every single magazine that I'd brought with me and they were supposed to last me for the whole week. I was just consoling myself with the thought that at least I'd be able to catch up with my mates once we were in our tent and then we could have a whole week together, when Mrs Blobby stood up and pulled down the microphone from above the driver's seat.

But, the second she started to speak, Spud woke up and – oh my God! What an embarrassment. It was as though he'd been plugged into the National Grid and ten thousand volts of electricity were being pumped through his body. He suddenly sprang to his feet and began jiggling around like a puppet on a string and thrashing his arm up and down in the air, like little kids do when they're in infant school.

'Oooo! Me, sir! Me, sir! I know, I know!' How nerdy is that? He even dreams about getting the answer right in class.

Mrs Blobby looked at him like he'd just been beamed down from another universe. 'Well, I'm pleased to see that you appear to have psychic abilities, Mr Pudmore, because I haven't asked any questions yet.'

Everyone turned round and started laughing at him. Talk about being socially challenged. On an embarrassment scale of one to ten, this was into the hundreds. I reached up and started pulling his jumper to try and make him sit down. Only he didn't sit down, he started to rummage around in the luggage rack above his head, pretending he was looking for something.

'I'm waiting!' Mrs Blobby bellowed – honestly, I don't know why she needed a microphone.

And then while he was scrabbling about in the luggage rack, Spud only went and knocked open the flight case that Auntie Venice had lent me (the one with the dodgy clasp) and all my emergency travel essentials fell out all over the coach. I so wanted to dig a hole and bury myself in it. There was mascara and lip-gloss and my hairbrush (and all sorts of other unmentionable things) rolling about the floor of the coach. But then, the worst possible scenario – my diary fell out! I went to grab it but we rounded a corner and it slid across the aisle. I lurched over to reach it but the coach started to climb a steep hill. I fell off the edge of the seat and everything, including my diary, went hurtling along the floor to the back.

'Sam Pudmore, sit down and Magenta Orange, sit up!' screamed The Blob.

But it was too late – who only went and picked up my diary but Kara Cow-face. She was holding it up and pretending to read from it with this smug grin on her face.

'Anyone for a bedtime story, lads?' she said, waving my diary in the air.

'Hey!' I yelled. 'Give that back.'

But The Great Beached Blob had got it in for me (just for a change – not!). 'If I have to tell you again, Magenta Orange, you will be sharing a tent with *me* for the week. Now, sit down.'

'But, miss . . .'

'Now!'

I sat down and Spud sat next to me. That woman is so unreasonable.

'Oh wow, I think I must've dozed off for a while,' Spud said.

'Dozed off?' Can you believe him? 'Durr! You've only been unconscious for the entire journey, woken up and made a complete prat of yourself and then totally ruined my life!' I snapped. 'You are so dumped!'

Then I turned round and glared at Kara. 'If you dare to open that . . .' I mouthed at her but she just tucked it down the front of her top and then gave it a little pat. Just you wait till we get off this coach – I am so going to get my own back on her.

'But, Magenta.' Spud was sulking. 'I really like you.'

I made my thumbs and first fingers into V shapes and then held up both hands to make a W. 'Whatever!' I said and turned my back on my newly exed.

'Now,' Mrs Blobby went on. 'Mr Snowdon is going to read out the pairs to share tents.'

Pairs? Could my week get any worse? I'd just assumed that Seema, Arlette and I would be sharing in a three. We'd be able to do the whole sleepover thing and that was the only thing keeping me interested in this stupid camp idea. It never occurred to me that one of them might have to share with someone else. I know they're both my mates and I'd hoped that I'd never have to choose between them but, secretly, if I had to choose, it would probably be Arl. Between you and me, Seema is a tad tidy for my liking.

Mr Snowdon stood up and took over the microphone. 'OK, listen up. We've tried to keep friends together as far as we can but sometimes it's just not possible. So if you're really not happy with the person we've paired you up with, then you can swap amongst yourselves but you must let us know.' Oooo, he is sooo gorgeous. Honestly, I'm going to do whatever activities Mr Snowdon's leading when we get there. 'Now, just for a change,' he continued, 'we'll start with the boys.' There was a groan from all the girls. 'Chad Albright and Angus Lyle, Daniel Davis and Sam Pudmore . . .'

'Whoa!' Spud suddenly stopped sulking and leaped to his feet again. 'No way!'

'Sort it out amongst yourselves,' Mr Snowdon said, before carrying on with his list. 'Hari Gulati and Delroy Walker, James Harper and . . .'

Then Spud turned to the back row and mouthed to Angus Lyle, 'Wanna swap partners?'

Honestly, boys are so immature. I wish Spud and Daniel would just get over themselves and forget this stupid jealousy thing they've got going. I mean, I know I said I'd prefer to share with Arlette but it doesn't matter to me if I get Seema, I won't throw a complete wobbler about it. I'll be mature whichever way it goes.

I turned round to look at the back seat and saw Chad Albright lean forwards towards Daniel. 'Hey, Danno. Looks like it's you and me – tent-buddies!'

'Whatever,' Daniel shrugged. Honestly, he is being grumpier than Grumpy McGrump at the moment. I mean there's no excuse for being so rude to Chad when he was only trying to be friendly.

The boys' list seemed to take for ever but eventually we got to the girls. Mrs Blobby stood up and went through it. '. . . Mia Hall and Sophie Simpson; Arlette Jackson and Seema Karia . . .'

What! Arlette and Seema together! What about me? Maybe I'd misheard her but when I turned round to look at my supposed mates, they were hugging each other like they'd been separated at birth and had only just found each other again. They didn't even look remotely sad that I wasn't going to be with them. I turned back to face The Blob. This was awful. I had my fingers firmly crossed that maybe I'd be in with Chelsea or Hattie and at least we could make a four and perhaps swap tent-partners halfway through the week or something.

But then, '. . . Kara Kennedy and Magenta

Orange . . .' No way! This was my worst ever nightmare scenario. A week in a confined space with that muscle-bound cow was totally inhuman. I'd rather live in a cave with the bog-monster for a month than spend an hour with Kara Kennedy – even in Buckingham Palace, never mind a tent.

I know Mrs Blobby doesn't like me, but this was vindictive beyond words. I was frantically looking round the coach for someone to swap partners with. I caught Chelsea's eye but then, '. . . Hattie Pringle and Chelsea Riordan . . .' The Blob continued, which totally ruined my Plan B. Then Hattie and Chelsea started hugging each other. It was like the whole coach had suddenly embarked on some humungous hug-fest which totally excluded me. My only consolation was that from the look on Kara's face she was as peed off about the arrangement as I was.

'I'm really hurt, you know, Magenta,' Spud said, when The Blob had finally sat down.

'*You're* hurt!' Spud can be so selfish sometimes. 'How do you think I feel?' I asked. 'I'm going into Camp Doom against my will, with only half my essential needs and I'm expected to share with that . . . that . . .'

'No,' Spud interrupted, looking like a puppy that'd had its tail trodden on. 'I mean, I'm hurt about us.'

'Spud, there is no us.' I rest my case about him being selfish. Didn't he realise what had just happened – that I'd been sentenced to seven days of torture in the company of Noxious Nora?

Just then Kara Kennedy stormed up the aisle of the coach towards the front. 'I'm getting this changed,' she said as she passed our seat.

'Well, don't think I'm exactly over the moon about it, either,' I called, crawling over the top of Spud to follow her. If, by some fluke, she managed to persuade The Blob to change her mind, there was no way I was going to let her get all the credit for it.

By the time I got to the front, she was already in full flow and Mrs Blobby looked like a boil that was about to burst. 'Oh, believe me, Kara, I am never anything *but* serious. Now get back to your seat immediately.'

'But . . .'

'No buts. This arrangement was my idea because I thought you might be a good influence on Magenta . . .' A good influence! The cheek of the woman. ' . . . however, if this protest continues, I might have to reassess my opinion of you.'

And you should have seen Kara (brown-nose) Kennedy grovelling after that. 'Oh thank you, Mrs

Delaney. I do appreciate the responsibility you've given me.' I don't know about Spud feeling travel-sick, there was a pretty good chance that *I* might chuck any minute. 'I will do my utmost not to let you down.'

There was no way I was going to let her get away with this. 'Er, hello!' I said. 'But she's stolen my diary. I refuse to share a tent with someone who steals diaries.' Which is a totally reasonable point of view.

'I haven't stolen it,' Kara laughed. 'I simply picked it up to stop it getting trodden on when it fell on the floor. It's at the back and you can have it as soon as we get to camp.' Liar, Liar, tongue's on fire!

'I won't hear any more of this, Magenta. Calling someone a thief is a very serious accusation. Now both of you go back to your seats. We'll be at camp in about five minutes.'

'Of course, Mrs Delaney.' Kara was being so slimy I'm surprised she didn't skid all over the coach. 'After you, Magenta.' Puke, puke, puke!

As I was walking back to my seat, I was fuming. Not only had The Blob got me to camp under false pretences, she'd split me up from my friends, robbed me of half my clothes and now she'd saddled me with the Sports (non)Personality of the Year – plus she'd taken away my only means of contacting the outside world, so I couldn't even phone my dad to come and sort her out. Could my life get any worse?

'Move over,' I said to Spud when I got back to the seat. I must admit I did snap a bit, but I think I could be excused in the circumstances. But he didn't move. He just sat there looking at me. 'Spud! I said move over. I've got to sit down.'

Kara was getting impatient and trying to push past me.

'Back off!' I snapped at her as she barged her way through.

Then she turned and whispered in my ear. 'You'd better be very nice to me or I think Chad would be interested to hear what you wrote about him on May 12th.'

Oh my God! She'd been reading my diary already. My life *had* just got worse.

'You . . .'

But just at that movement, Spud stood up and hurled the contents of his packed lunch – all down my front! Gross!

'I told you I got travel-sick,' he moaned.

Brilliant! We're not even off the coach and already I'm an outfit down. I *knew* I needed more clothes. On the positive side though, Kara had taken the brunt of it (serves her right for pushing past me) so there is some justice in the world.

And now it's started to rain! Oh deep joy. I'm sure we just passed a sign that said 'Welcome to Hell'.

10
Magenta

I think the easiest way to tell you about my week at
Camp Calamity is just to let you read it for yourself
from my diary. Luckily (and believe me there haven't
been many lucky moments over the last week) while
Kara the Cruel was complaining to The Blob on the
way here, Daniel managed to sneak my diary out of
her bag. What a star! He gave it back to me just as we
were getting off the coach. He's definitely gone up
in my estimation again, although he's still walking
about with face like a wet weekend. I thought *I* was
miserable about camp but I'm nothing compared to
Daniel. Anyway, that's not my problem and at least
I've got my diary back. Here goes:

Monday
8 p.m.
Soon as we got here Blobby sent Kara & me off
to shower block to get cleaned up. Thought had
wandered into sheep-dip by mistake. Gross! Looked
like Stainless Steel City. Everywhere was horrible
metal. All scratched and dented. And showerhead

looked like something Gran puts on end of watering can when she weed-killers front path. Total health hazard.

Water hadn't had time to heat up yet (so man in reception said). Thought I was human pin-cushion being stuck with thousand pins of ice. But worse – had to wash my hair! Which meant all glitter got washed out. Not happy. How am I supposed to impress Chad when Great Blob has made me send home all hair products (except shampoo) & all lovely alluring evening wear – not forgetting that legs looked as though have just lost kicking match. Life v.v.v. unfair.

As if that not bad enough, all best pitches for tents had been taken by time we got out of shower. Had to walk halfway across Wales to edge of field before found anywhere. Miles from toilet block and reception building. Course, Kara never let me forget about it – was all, 'It's going to take us ages to get to breakfast every morning, because of you and your stupid boyfriend.' And, 'All the hot water'll have gone by the time we get to the showers, thanks to you.' Blamers Anonymous or what? Seems to have slipped her mind that *she* barged past me as Spud was in full flow – or full throw – ho ho! Idea of spending entire week with her not looking any more appealing. On positive side – being on edge of campsite means lovely view across valley – or at least, will probably be lovely view when rain stops.

When came to put up tent, more disasters. Had not only got worst pitch but had also won booby prize in tent stakes. By time we got out of showers, everyone else had been given equipment. All had state-of-the-art igloo tents with built-in ground sheet & bendy sticks that just push through little eyelets. V. trendy colours too with silver or gold trims. Looked really cool (well, when I say cool – all relative). But not us – oh no! Because we were last, ended up with orange nylon ridge tent. Looks like relic from Neolithic Boy Scout Jamboree.

Of course, soon as we started to put it up, teensy little breeze turned into howling gale. Every time tried to put canvas over metal poles, whole thing took off like enormous orange kite. V.v. dangerous. My super-supportive tent-mate let go so I was dragged towards edge of campsite and sharp drop down into field of cows. Only saved from near death on electric fence by quick thinking. Clung on to nylon and flung self forward on to ground with tent wrapped in arms. Phew!

Kara was all, 'Sorry, Magenta, but I thought it was

better to let go than to endanger our lives.' Yeah right! Save herself and leave me to float off across Irish Sea. Cow! Managed to get tent up (at long last) but then aluminium poles sprang apart & whole thing collapsed – five times! Grrr! Took us 2 hrs in end. Kara hurt finger and had to go to first-aid centre – said it might affect her serve in tennis!!!! (Drama Queen, or what?) Left me to put finishing details to tent. Felt v. proud of self.

Now need another shower and more clothes (as result of mud bath whilst saving tent). Plus, previously easily identifiable orange tent is now dingy brown because of rolling-in-mud episode.

Missed dinner due to tent taking so long to put up – and this is last meal that staff will be cooking. Have to fend for selves on food front from now on! Am wondering if starvation can happen in single week?

Staff v. kindly (not!) saved us a few measly lettuce leaves & a spoonful of grated cheese. Others got pizza & chips – grrr!

But at least stopped raining – yeah!
10 p.m.
By time got back to tent, it was in crumpled heap again. So not fair! No one told me that bits of string were called guy ropes and need to be tied to tent pegs. Thought they were washing lines. When Kara

went off and said, 'Don't forget the guys,' thought she was talking about Chad and Daniel.

And on positive note, human guys (Chad & Daniel) came over & helped us put it up again. Chad's been going to summer camp in USA since he was about nine & knew all about tent pegs. You should've seen him hammering them into ground with mallet – talk about fit! Took off his top and was just in shorts, swinging hammer down and whacking them into grass as sun was setting. Phwoar! Daniel quite sweet too – till Kara gave him slobbery kiss that made stomach turn – yuk! Must've felt like being smacked in mouth with wet fish. Don't know why he goes out with her. They've gone off for walk so have some time to self to write this.

11 p.m.

Am now in sleeping bag – know what caterpillars must feel like. No room to move and tent is also on slight slope so keep sliding down towards zip end. On bright side, still no rain. Who knows, maybe will wake up tomorrow and be like butterfly emerging from 13.5 tog cocoon ready for brand new day.

Tuesday
7 a.m.

Oh my God! Think steamroller must have come at

night and pummelled me all over. Every bone in body v.v. achy. Never mind waking up like butterfly – feel more like squashed moth.

Aaaaaagh! Something just fell out of my hair – and it moved! Ewww! This is so gross. Bad enough that I have to share tent with a prize cow, now also have to share sleeping bag with creepy-crawlies. Want to go home. Will do cooking and cleaning for a month. Will even wear Belinda's hideous bridesmaid dress. Want my dad. Want my phone back. Get me out of here!

8.30 a.m.

Hideous breakfast – burnt veggie sausages, burnt beans, burnt fried bread. Everything totally incinerated except tea & that was cold cos water took too long to boil. Am having cornflakes tomorrow.

Got back to tent to find Kara screaming at me. 'Move up a gear, Magenta, it's tent inspection in five minutes.'

Tent inspection? Wonder what that's about? Maybe it's health inspection to get rid of bugs – hope so. Have 5 gnat bites already.

10 p.m.

Tent inspection was not for creepy-crawlies. Was for tidiness and my half failed. Kara fuming. Means we were on washing-up tonight. On positive side, Kara not speaking to me.

Also, today was first day of activities. This place run as major dictatorship. Definitely specified did not want to take part in any activities involving getting hair wet. So, The Blob put me in two-person canoe with Kara the Kayaking Queen! She was flashing her paddles and flicking water up at me all day. Didn't matter tho' because raining again today so would've got wet whatever activity. Not quite as wet as when saw Chad on horseback trotting along side of lake looking like some gorgeous cowboy on way to rid entire town of evil bandits. Put down paddle to wave at him but paddle slipped off side of kayak into water. Oops! Tried to reach out to grab it and ended up demonstrating capsized drill in middle of lake. Instructor had to come out to rescue us. Another reason Kara not speaking to me. Apparently points given each day and prizes awarded at end of week. Kara and I currently bottom of league.

Gnat bites have increased to 12 – mainly on facial area – hideous.

Wednesday
8.45 a.m.
Blob is v.v. horrible. Only had two pairs of socks, hairbrush, lip-gloss & T-shirt on sleeping bag at inspection and she called it a fail. On washing-up

again tonight! Nails already seriously ruined. Think this is victimisation. Wonder if I can sue school? Our group on pony trekking today. Hope it's better than canoeing.

5 p.m.

Ponies *not* cute little things that live in dream castles with long flowing manes and magical powers like played with when little. Are mean, mean animals. Mine called Snowy but should be renamed Satan! It almost amputated my fingers when only trying to be nice and feed it carrots. Then, on 'gentle walk' through hills (in reality, bottom-numbing, thigh-splitting, bone-jarring torture session) Satan had brainstorm & bolted away from group. Was screaming for help but everyone just laughing. V.v. embarrassed. Ended up in lake then Satan decided to have drink and tipped me over his head, straight into water! Am seeing way too much of lake this week. Also running out of clothes v. quickly.

9.30 p.m.

Supposed to have 'bonfire baked potatoes' for dinner. Meant had to eat cinders – disgusting! Hate this place. Will look like Stick-Girl by end of week.

Blob's idea of recreation tonight was quiz night. Grabbed Chad to be on our team – yeah! Were tying with another team so had tie-breaker question,

'Where is the alimentary canal?' I shouted out, 'South America!' Chad and rest of team not impressed. Kara v. rude. 'Grow a brain, Magenta!' How is anyone with decent social life supposed to know stupid facts like that?

V. cold and v. hungry. Am going to bed now. Kara gone to see Daniel so at least have some peace. Gnat bites multiplying. Look like have got measles.

11 p.m.

Kara came back in strop. Asked if she wanted to talk but said she'd rather talk to the cows in the field. Evil smell in tent – feel sick. Oh my God! Kara only trod in cowpat on way back from seeing Daniel – ewwww! Have to stop writing now so she can have torch to clean up – yuk!

Thursday

Kara spent half night cleaning out tent. On positive side, wasn't my fault we failed tent inspection today. Still have to do washing-up tho'!

Activity is orienteering today. Not sure what that is. Know that Orient means far east. Maybe going to be taken out for a Chinese?

Friday

Orienteering so *not* about egg fried rice! Although

did almost end up in far east. Were given map, compass and instructions and dumped in middle of forest. Was in group with Arl & Seema, which was good but also had Kara Bossy-boots with us. Think I must have been evil ogre in previous life to deserve this.

Compass is totally stupid instrument. Thought it was supposed to tell us which way to go, but think ours must've been broken because it always pointed same direction – useless. Had argument with control-freak Kennedy (who said I had map wrong way round – as if!). She said we'd passed same stile three times but sure it was three different ones – all stiles look alike to me. She tried to pull map out of my hands but it ripped. (Ooops!) Then, even worse, my half blew away.

All went horribly wrong from then on. Arlette crying. Kara sulking. Seema trying to light fire with twigs and flints in style of Native Americans to try and make smoke signal & attract attention. Soon as she got it lit, started raining again. Then mist came down. V.v. scary.

Search and rescue helicopter found us about midnight.

But on positive side – it meant we missed washing-up yesterday. And also, spent last night in sick bay –

oh yes – decent bed & proper food! Have also been allowed today off to rest and recover! Yeah!

Daniel came up to see me this morning. Thought Chad might have come with him but didn't. Never mind, still got tomorrow to win him round. Daniel dumped Kara (that's why she was in strop) – thought he'd be happy to be rid of her but still acting like Groucho the Grouchy. Sweet of him to come tho'.

Saturday
8 a.m.
Last full day – yes! Am doing rock-climbing and abseiling with Mr Snowdon today. Chad also in my group. Can't wait – 2 hunks in one session. Lovely way to end week of hell. Teensy bit worried as cliff is 30 metres high but on positive side – is not raining and sun's out. Will wear best sun-top to impress Chad.
8 p.m.
Worst day ever! Not only did sun-top reveal full extent of gnat-attack (look like victim of bubonic plague) but also discovered Chad is not nice person.

Spent morning on climbing wall in main building – easy peasy, lemon squeezy. Then after lunch (at least sandwiches can't get burned) went in minibus into mountain bit. Had all proper gear – harnesses and everything. V. uncomfortable implements of torture. No wonder ponies such evil animals when all trussed up with girths & saddles & stuff. Have decided to forgive Snowy for dumping me in lake. Realise must be in mega discomfort all the time.

First of all climbed up rock face – no probs! Was quite impressed with self, actually. Move over Lara Croft! Then had to get down again – v.v. scary. Mr Snowdon v. fit in climbing gear – standing at top of cliff looking totally gorge. Woman (although looks more like man/Teletubby) from Centre went down and waited at bottom. Bit worried but thought she was probably strong enough to catch me if necessary. If not, big enough to act like crash mat & break fall.

Chad went first. Zooming down rope like Spiderman. Teletubby woman had to pull rope & put brake on to slow him down. Serves him right – show-off. Course Kara had to go next. Then others. Only me left.

Felt bit queasy, standing at top looking down. Mr Snowdon clipped me on to rope and made me lean out at 90° to rock face. Aaaaagh! Kept telling me to relax so rope would slide through hand. How supposed to relax when just about to meet certain death?

Mr S tried to prise fingers open but locked tight on rope. 'Relax, Magenta!' Didn't matter how many times said it, did not make it any easier to stop thinking of self like raspberry jam splattered all over ground. 'Just keep taking deep breaths,' he said. Great advice! Took such deep breaths that started to hyperventilate – made situation 6 squillion times worse – went into spasm & couldn't move single muscle.

Mega fear factor – 30 metres above ground, lying out parallel to rocky floor, suspended by thread, not able to move. Mr S had to pull me back up.

Tellytubby woman went back to minibus, got paper bag, climbed back up cliff and made me breathe into bag. Mr S said to call it a day. Tellytubby woman said to go down with her – no way! Did not trust teensy little rope to hold two people. Tried to back away but walked into thorn bush and added three thousand scratches to already mutilated body (due to midge bites).

Finally convinced Mr S & Tinky Winky that was well enough for another go. This time did it – yeah! But, as lowering self down cliff, noticed pink thread running alongside rope. Same colour as best sun-top. What a coincidence!

Realised true horror of situation when almost on

ground. Thread had caught on thorn bush and sun-top was unravelling in front of very eyes (also in front of very eyes of entire group – including Chad!). When got to ground was reduced to straps only. Rest of best sun-top was dangling down cliff face. Was left standing in bra and harness.

Kara saying, 'Get a grip, Magenta. We all read your diary. We know you only came to camp because you fancy the pants off Chad, but don't you think this is going a bit too far?' Wanted to die.

Chad (slimeball) was all, 'I don't ever recall saying I wanted to see more of you, Magenta – especially this much.' Everyone laughing. Total humiliation.

Daniel took off own T-shirt and gave it to me – bless. Is so sweet. Shame didn't work out between us. Sat with me in minibus all way back. Kara fuming. Saying, 'Some people will do anything to gain attention.' Should have put her sleeping bag in field next door with rest of herd.

Leaving disco tonight. Everyone in shower block getting ready. Am not going.
10.30 p.m.
Won a prize! Yeah!

Daniel dragged me off to disco. Was OK. Had award ceremony before started. Most of activity prizes went to Chad & Cow-face. Seema & Arl won

153

tidiest tent. Daniel won one for best orienteering group and Angus Lyle won best at lighting campfire (go figure!).

Right at end had award for most entertaining person at camp and guess what? Was me! V.v. proud of self. First time have won anything.

Now raining again tho'! Still, going home tomorrow. Can't wait.

Sunday
3.30 a.m.
Oh my God! End of world! Either that or have sleepwalked into shower block. Have just woken up with icy cold water dripping on head.

Sleeping bag is like giant sponge – soaking wet. Gross squelching sound every time move. Yuk! Just put hand on floor of tent and is like swimming-pool. Water everywhere.

Thunder and lightning outside like something out of Frankenstein film. Kara still asleep. Am shining torch about and can see top of tent bowed in like humungous orange water balloon. Looks like just about to burst.

Uh-oh! Something v. scary happening. Feels like am sliding down tent towards zip end again. Wait a sec. Is not me sliding down tent – is tent sliding down slope! Help! Is gaining speed. Must get out before end up fried on electric fence. Heeeeeeeeelp!

11
Daniel

I was DJ-ing and the club was rammed. Magenta was dancing right in front of the DJ box and she looked so beautiful. Lights were flashing and her eyes were sparkling. She was smiling at me with that lovely, sweet smile of hers.

'Heeeeeeeeeelp!'

Suddenly, people in kilts were clamouring to get close to the decks. They were rushing me – bagpipes and haggises were flying everywhere. Mum was in the box too and she was just standing there watching as Magenta was sucked into the sea of tartan. The love of my life was being swallowed up, getting further and further away, and then suddenly the crowd morphed into a humungous shoal of fish, leaping up at me.

'Heeeeeeeeeelp!' I could hear Magenta's distant cry as she disappeared from my view and my life for ever – while my mother, the traitor, just patted me on the back and told me how well I was doing.

'Noooo!' I woke up with the sleeping bag wrapped round me so tightly that it felt like I was being crushed to death by an enormous nylon boa constrictor.

'Jeez, Danno – give me a break!' Chad poked his head out of his sleeping bag. 'It would've been nice to've had at least one decent night's sleep this week without you having the heebie-jeebies.'

Can you believe the creep? I wriggled myself round so that my sleeping bag unwound and I could at least breathe properly. Then I groped around for the torch and shone it straight into his eyes – you know, like MI6 do when they're interrogating a suspected double agent.

'I know this is quite a complex concept for you to grasp, Chad, but not everything in this universe revolves round you.' I could see him screwing up his eyes as I flashed the torch from one eye to the other. 'Strange as it might seem, I haven't been having nightmares just to give you a hard time. As paybacks come, that would be pretty warped, if not totally masochistic!'

'Well, if you take my advice, you'll get some serious therapy when you get home.' And then the moron rolled over and went back to sleep.

What a prat! Like I needed a psychologist to tell me what was going on in my head. Although to be fair to him, I hadn't actually told anyone that I was going to be whisked off to the land of Rangers and Celtic and the Loch Ness monster. I lay back, listening to the rain pounding on the tent and the ominous rumble of distant thunder.

I decided that it had probably done me good being at camp this week. Apart from the obvious – like getting me away from my barracuda-featured brother – it had given me some space from the starry-eyed geriatric lovers (gross! I wish I could get that image out of my head). At least at camp Mum couldn't try to brainwash me into wanting to grab my sporran and do a Highland fling at the opportunities the clean air and Scottish education system would offer me. Here I've had the chance to do some serious thinking and re-evaluate my situation – with particular emphasis on the whole Magenta issue.

OK, I know I said that I'd rather just be friends with her than not have anything to do with her at all, but actually what I've discovered this week is that that's not true. Maybe if we'd never gone out at all, it wouldn't matter, I'd be OK to carry on as mates because, like they say, you don't miss what you've never had. But we *have* been out together – twice – and both times it was amazingly, mind-blowingly, wonderfully, ecstatically brilliant! There's no way I can possibly face going back to how we were before. It would be like taking a starving kid, sitting him down in front of the biggest, most mouth-watering, deep pan meat-feast pizza and then, when he's only halfway through the first slice, taking it away again and making him sit and watch while everyone else stuffs themselves stupid. No way was I going to let that happen.

So, I've had some time this week to get my head together and really weigh up all sides. And believe me, it hasn't been easy.

Take the staying-with-Dad option – on the positive side:

1) I'd still get to see Magenta sometimes and we might be able to go out together again, although there's no way it would be the same as when we were going out before and she was just next door. (So that takes me back to the whole pizza/starving child thing.)

2) I'd get to know Dad better and do some father/son bonding, which would be really cool.

But on the other hand, there are some humungous problems with the whole staying-down-here-and-living-with-Dad idea:

1) Dad lives right out of town so, even if I managed to wangle it that I could stay at

Archimedes High, I would only see Magenta at breaktime and lunch-time. I wouldn't be able to just go over the balcony to talk to her and do stuff like we do now.

2) If I went to Dad's, I'd still have to put up with Joe – BIG downer!

3) There's the added irritation factor of Dad's latest girlfriend, Pauline, and her four kids. Pauline's got a laugh like a constipated donkey and her kids go from six to twelve and they're all girls and all like Pauline's mini-me. Usually when Joe and I go there, they're at their dad's, but sometimes we clash and it does my brain in, even for a weekend.

4) And this sounds awful – but since Dad left when I was little, I've only seen him every other weekend and for the odd week in the summer. I mean, don't get me wrong, Dad's great but it's just that there are whole chunks of my life where he hasn't featured.

5) I'd only see Mum every now and then – for the odd week of the holidays. And, I know I'm mad at her right now, but most of the time she's really cool and I know I'd miss her like crazy.

So, if I stayed at Dad's it would be like starting

over with a whole new life – new parent, new house, new neighbourhood, new step-brats.

And then, of course, there's the other side of the situation. If I go to Scotland with Mum and The Duck, I'd hardly ever see Dad and there'd be all the starting over stuff up there too. And, this could be the real decider: I'd probably never see Magenta again.

What do I do? I know missing her would be one of the most painful things I could ever imagine – even worse than pulling out my own teeth with tweezers, but would it be any less painful staying at Dad's and only seeing her part time and risk having to watch her go out with other boys?

You see, this week, every time I caught sight of her with Spud (which wasn't often to be honest – not after he hurled all over her on the way here) or Chad, or any other boy she spoke to, it felt like she'd plunged a red-hot sword into my chest, gouged out my heart, minced it into a thousand tiny pieces and then tossed it to the birds to peck at.

What a decision to have to make! If I go to Scotland, I've got the dental extractions, but if I stay here I've got open-heart surgery – all without anaesthetic. Whichever way you look at it, I'm in for some serious pain. No wonder I've been having nightmares. And I couldn't help thinking what a pity it was that I wasn't having these bad dreams while I was at home. At least then Mum would be suffering too. Instead of which she's living it up with The Duck while I'm being deprived of one of my basic needs. You'd think that when she made her totally selfish decision to go gallivanting off to the end of the world with her geriatric sugar daddy, she would've known the effect this would have on me. Doesn't she realise that sleep deprivation is one of the key elements of torture?

I sat up and looked for my watch: three thirty-five – great! Then suddenly, above the noise of the rain I heard, 'Heeeeeeeelp!' again. Only this time, I wasn't asleep, so it couldn't have been in my dream.

'Heeeeeeeeeelp!' Uh-oh. It was Magenta's voice – I'd know it anywhere.

My heart started racing. Suddenly, all my worries seemed minor compared with Magenta being in trouble. I scrabbled out of my sleeping bag, unzipped the tent door and poked my head out. It was peeing down and suddenly lightning flashed like some huge floodlight illuminating the entire campsite. Did I say the thunder was distant? Well, it must've suddenly gone on to warp factor ten because there was an almighty crash right overhead. Whoa! We were in a field in the middle of a major thunderstorm. This was seriously dangerous and it was very clear to me that Magenta must be terrified.

Magenta and Kara's tent was about fifty metres away, right at the far end of the campsite. They'd got one of the old-fashioned tents in bright orange, so I could see it clearly every time the lightning flashed. The weird thing was though, with every flash of lightning, it seemed to be getting further away. I rubbed my eyes, thinking it must be some sort of weird optical illusion or the result of sleep deprivation. But then I realised – it *was* getting further away. Oh no! Their tent was slipping down the field. And about twenty metres away was an escarpment that fell away into a field of cows.

'Heeeeeelp!'

I went back into the tent and grabbed the torch and my Leatherman, which is this really cool technician's multi-tool that Mum had given me as a double present last term. Part of it was for doing so well in the stage crew and part of it was a get well gift when I broke my leg rescuing Magenta. It's a bit like a Swiss army knife only it's got more gadgets on it (like pliers and stuff) and it doesn't have the thing for taking stones out of horses' hooves. It's also way more manly.

'Now what?' Chad snapped. 'Can't a guy get *any* sleep around here?'

'Magenta's in trouble,' I said, scrabbling around to take my Leatherman out of its carrying pouch. 'Listen . . .' You could just make out her cry of, '*Save me!*' above the storm.

Chad rolled over in his sleeping bag again. 'Probably just broken a nail.'

What a prize plonker! I crawled to the entrance and stepped out into the torrential rain.

'Hey! Fasten that up. It's freezing in here,' Chad snarled.

But I was in too much of a hurry to worry about him. I set off across the field as fast as I could. Mum had bought me a new pair of pyjamas to bring to camp but who wears PJs any more? Anyone knows that the only thing manly men wear in bed is boxers and a T-shirt so that's all I'd got on, although, I must admit, I was beginning to regret it – it was freezing out there. The rain was pelting down and the whole field seemed to have been turned into a massive bog. I was squelching through the mud, tripping over guy ropes and crashing into tents as the lightning flashed and the thunder roared round me almost continuously. But I knew I had to get to Magenta.

Mr Snowdon's voice came over a loudhailer.

'Everyone make your way to reception. Leave all your personal belongings.'

People were starting to emerge from their tents and run towards the main building with cagoules over their heads but I kept going in the opposite direction. I was starting to panic. Magenta's tent was sliding away from me quite quickly now. It seemed as though the tent pegs had come out because the guy ropes were waving in the wind and the fly-sheet was flapping at either side of the tent like a pair of giant orange wings.

'HEEEEEEEELLLLLPPPPP!' Magenta's screams were getting louder.

In the nanosecond that the lightning flashed, I could make out the silhouette of two people near the far end of the tent and they seemed to be struggling with the zip.

'It's OK – I'm here!' I called, but I don't know if she could hear me.

My vest and boxers were sticking to me with the rain, and the mud had splashed up at me as I'd been running. I'd forgotten to put on any shoes too, so my feet looked like the creature from the deep but I didn't care. There was only one thing on my mind and that was saving Magenta before she tumbled down the escarpment and a drop of nearly two metres on to the electric fence at the bottom.

At last I reached her tent. I grabbed one of the guy ropes that was waving in its wake and pulled. But all that did was yank off the fly-sheet! The main tent carried on sliding away from me. I ran after it, but where the tent had careered across the soggy grass, the ground was well slippery. My feet were slithering all over the place and a couple of times I fell over into the mud. I couldn't believe what was happening. This was even worse than my nightmares!

I lurched forwards and managed to catch hold of the tent.

'Magenta, I'm here!' I shouted.

'Daniel – the zip's stuck!' she screamed. 'We're going to die!'

'Don't worry,' I called.

But the weight of the two girls inside was more than me and it carried on gaining momentum and pulling me along with it! I dropped my torch and, with one hand clutching the tent, I pulled out my Leatherman. Using my teeth, I flicked open the knife with the serrated blade and slashed open the back of the tent.

'Quick!' I yelled above the thunder. 'Get out!'

But the next thing I knew, Kara had pushed Magenta to the ground and was scrambling over the top of her to get out of the tent. She jumped out and flung her arms round my neck, knocking me off balance and making me lose my grip on the tent.

'Oh, Daniel, thank you so much,' she was saying. 'You're so wonderful.'

'Whoa!' I said, peeling her arms off my neck and pushing her to one side. 'Magenta's still in there!'

'Well! I was only trying to say thank you. How ungrateful can you . . .'

But I didn't wait to hear whatever it was she was saying. I ran forwards just in time; the tent had got to the edge of the escarpment. I reached out my hand and grabbed hold of Magenta's outstretched arm. She was looking up at me with those gorgeous eyes. Oh, she looked so cute and vulnerable peering out of the rip in the tent – and her hand looked so tiny and dainty. But also, surprisingly strong because she clasped hold of my arm with such a grip that I thought my circulation might be cut off. But I didn't even flinch as I pulled her out of the ripped tent – just as it toppled over the edge.

'Wow, Daniel, you are such a hero!' she said, peering down the escarpment on to the mangled heap of nylon and aluminium at the bottom. 'That was soooo close!'

Yeeees! Magenta had said I was a hero! I wanted to

punch the air and jump up and down. Instead, I said, calmly, 'Come on, you ought to get inside. You've had a shock, you need to get into the warm.' I was aching to put my arms round her and wrap her up and protect her for ever.

'Ahem!' Suddenly, Kara was standing in front of us with her hands on her hips. 'Excuse me interrupting this touching little moment you two losers are sharing but my trainers are in that tent.'

'And?' I couldn't believe she was going on about her trainers when I'd probably just saved her life.

'Have you any idea how much those trainers cost? They aren't just ordinary trainers, you know.'

And then Magenta stood up to her. 'No, they're not ordinary trainers, they're stupid trainers. And what's even more stupid than your trainers? You, Kara! You are the most stupid person I've ever met because you tied your stupid trainers to the zip of our tent and it's your stupid fault we were nearly killed.'

'I tied them there for security!' Kara said, sarcastically.

'Well, they're secure now, aren't they? Come on, Daniel, let's go and get dry.' And she linked her arm through mine and we headed for the reception area. I felt so proud of her.

'Everyone inside immediately!' Mr Snowdon's voice boomed out again.

As we headed for the main building, Magenta clutched my arm and snuggled up to me. It was the most amazing feeling.

'I thought you were brilliant, you know, Daniel,' Magenta was saying as we ran towards the building. The thunderstorm was still raging all round us and people were running about in their pyjamas; some of the girls were crying (and one or two of the boys too).

'Thanks,' I said, taking off my T-shirt and putting it over her head. Not that it was much use – it was about as dry as a soggy dish-cloth, but I thought at least it might keep some of the rain off her.

'You're so sweet,' she said. And then she stopped and looked up at me. It felt like someone had just lit the blue touch-paper in my stomach and the fireworks of love were bursting into action. 'And I just want you to know that I'm really sorry about the whole Chad thing.'

Him again! Grrr! 'Don't even go there. It's history.'

I led her inside where they were giving out foil blankets to keep people warm. And the staff had opened up the kitchen and made some soup. It turns out that half the hillside had turned into a giant mudslide and loads of tents had lost their pegs and slipped forwards. Most of them hadn't gone any further than the tent in front, but because Magenta's was right on the edge, there was nothing to stop it.

'I just want you to know that I only did it because it was for charity,' she went on, sipping her soup and looking so cosy and twinkly in her foil blanket.

'It's OK, really, let's leave it,' I said, beginning to feel a tad tetchy. After all, I'd just rescued her and I wanted a few minutes to bask in her company without Chad Albright sticking his gleaming incisors in. Anyway, I bet she didn't know that he wears a retainer at night and he's such a poseur that he even has his initials in gold on the box where he keeps it in the day. What a saddo!

Just then Mr Snowdon came up. 'Daniel, I've just heard about what you did and I'd like to congratulate you on your bravery.'

'It was nothing, sir,' I said, trying not to look too pleased with myself but hoping Magenta was taking it all in.

'Oh yes, sir,' she cut in. 'Daniel is amazingly brave. This is the second time he's saved my life.' I felt myself going a deep shade of beetroot. 'He really is the best friend anyone could wish for.' And she gave me a little peck on the cheek.

Can you believe it? A measly little peck on the

cheek – after all I'd done for her! And what was all that about being her friend? I'd just saved her life – again! But it was obvious that as far as Magenta's concerned, that meant nothing. All I was ever going to be in her eyes was 'Daniel my mate next door'. She was never going to be able to think of me romantically.

'Hey, Magenta, are you OK?' Chad Mr Gleaming-teeth Albright had come over. 'I said there was never a dull moment with you around.'

They both laughed and the silver of Chad's blanket glinted in Magenta's eye. There it was – Excalibur right through my heart! I knew then that I could never bear to be with her on a part-time basis. I was definitely an all-or-nothing man. So it would be less painful for me in the long run to have nothing.

At that moment, standing in the centre's kitchen, with a chipped mug of watery tomato soup in my hand, I made my decision. I was going to go to Scotland.

12
Magenta

My life is totally ruined! The last six weeks since I got back from camp have been the worst – EVER!

1) I got my SATs results which, personally speaking, considering all the trauma I've been going through this year, I thought weren't too bad. Unfortunately, call me telepathic, but I just knew Dad wasn't going to let it go when he saw them. Something to do with the fact that his nostrils flared out like a pair of black holes, threatening to suck in everything within the gravitational pull of a small planet!

2) After twenty-seven renditions of his whole, 'you'll never get anywhere in life/end up living in a cardboard box' routine, I now have to go to a private tutor every single Saturday for the rest of my life. He's called Mr Dumbarton (I call him The Dung-beetle) – and he's gross! He has skin like orange peel that's been left out for about a month and eyebrows that meet in the middle. And he gives me homework – on top

of the homework I get from school! Life is so unfair!

3) My dad refused to even look at my gorgeous bridesmaid dress design that would've made me look like a radically cool princess. Instead, he did a passable impersonation of the Incredible Hulk, saying that attending his wedding was not a matter for debate; I was going and I was wearing whatever Belinda wanted me to wear – end of! Must make a mental note to look up the Children's Act on the computer in the library. It's all very well the government giving children rights but it seems that nobody's told the parents!

And,

4) Probably the worst thing that has ever happened to me (except for my mum dying, but I can't remember much about that) – Daniel is moving!

I couldn't believe it when we got home from camp and there was a For Sale board outside his house.

'You mean to tell me you've known for a whole week and you didn't say a word?' I asked when I went over the balcony to his room that night.

He nodded. He was lying on his bed, with his hands behind his head, staring up at the ceiling and his stupid poster of Sarah Michelle Gellar, which, by the way, is looking seriously in need of replacement these days.

'So when exactly *were* you going to tell me?'

He shrugged. 'Dunno.'

Some friend he turned out to be! 'You know what, Daniel – I tell you everything! Every little thing that goes on in my life I come round here and run it past you . . .'

'I know,' he said.

'All the stuff with Belinda and Dad . . .'

'I know.'

'All the stuff with my SATs . . .'

He sighed.

'Then something as major as this happens and you decide to keep it all to yourself. I mean, how does that work, Daniel?'

'Look, I know I should probably've talked to you about it . . .' he started.

'Too right, you should've talked to me about it!' I was getting really peed off with him. I mean, you think you know someone and then they go and treat you like that. 'I thought we were supposed to be friends again.'

And that was it! He suddenly sprang off his bed and started to shout at me – I mean really shout. I know he's been a bit annoyed with me in the past and we've had little squabbles but this was mega decibel stuff.

'And that's all it'll ever be to you, isn't it, Magenta? Friends! Well you can take your stupid friendship and stuff it!' Whoa! 'I don't need it any more. Because, you know what?' He was walking towards me and I started to back away towards the French window because if I thought my dad could morph into Hulk mode at the drop of a grade, then he had nothing on Daniel that night. 'I'm going to make a new start – with new friends. Friends who know the meaning of the word.' And his point? 'It obviously escaped your notice last week, Magenta, but your *friend* – i.e. me – was having a major personal crisis . . .'

'You didn't say,' I offered in my defence.

'No,' he said, suddenly sinking down on to the bed again. 'A true friend wouldn't need to be told. I rest my case.' Then he looked straight at me and his eyes looked really sad. Normally, Daniel's got quite nice eyes – his eyelashes curl up and they look really cute – but just then they seemed flat and dull. 'I'd like to be on my own now, please,' he finished.

I wasn't sure what to do. 'OK,' I said, a teensy bit nervously; I'd never seen him like this before. And then I added, 'But you know I'm always here for you.'

'Yeah, right!' he said and rolled over with his back to me. 'Shut the French window on your way out.'

And that was probably the last proper conversation we had – although I use the word conversation in the loosest possible sense of the word. I mean he did apologise the next day, and he still says 'Hi' and 'Bye' and stuff, but that's about all. To be fair, though, it hasn't all been because he was in a strop, it's mainly because he's hardly been around since we got home. He's been going up and down to Scotland with Mary looking at fish farms and new schools. And then they went up a couple of weeks ago for Mary to get married to this guy she'd met at the hospital. Joe didn't go – it was just Daniel and this Donald bloke's grown-up kids. Mary came round and showed us the photographs one night.

So, there I was, the Thursday before the end of term. In theory, I should've been over the moon: I was one day away from the six-week break, Belinda and I had made up, it was almost my birthday and I was going to be a bridesmaid on Saturday. I should have been floating on clouds. But, there was this huge dark shadow of gloom that made all the happy events seem like nothing by comparison – Mary and

Daniel were having their leaving party that night. They weren't actually moving until Monday but, because of everything else that was happening, Mary thought it would be best this way.

It was Sports Day and Arlette and I were sitting on the grass at the edge of the playing-field. Seema was in the final of the high jump so she was over in the competitors' area but Arl and I were spectators – or not, if you're going to be strictly accurate about the definition of the word spectator.

'You can still write and phone, you know – Scotland's not the end of the world,' Arlette said, after I'd been going on and on about how unfair Daniel had been about this whole moving business.

'It won't be the same, though.' I was feeling as though someone had filled a giant balloon with cement and stuffed it into the middle of my chest. 'I mean, it's practically like he's part of the furniture. He's always been there. All I had to do was pop across the balcony and – *hello, Daniel!* Just like that.'

But, before I could say anything else, Magnus and Spud came up to us. Magnus was carrying the school camcorder and Spud had an enormous card in his hand.

'We're making a video for Danno to take with him

to Scotland. You know, where all his mates say nice things about him,' Magnus said.

'We're going to give it to him at the party tonight,' Spud added, waving this humungous card around.

'Ooo, that's a brilliant idea. I'll say some nice things,' Arlette said, turning to face the camera.

'Great!' Magnus put the camera to his eye.

Spud started acting like some big-shot film director. 'And – action!' He flapped the card closed in front of the lens like a clapperboard.

Arlette flicked her hair back from her eyes and smiled. 'I just want to say that, Daniel, I think you're the hunkiest boy in the whole school – in fact you're tastier than a packet of Jaffa Cakes and I'm going to miss you like crazy.' Then she slapped her hand over her mouth and gasped. 'He's not going to actually watch this at the party, is he? He won't see this till after he's gone?'

'And cut!' Spud said, wafting the card in front of the camera again.

'Nooooo!' squealed Arlette. 'Let me record it again. Promise me you'll edit it out.'

'OK,' Magnus said, pointing the camera at me.

'Ehem!' Spud cleared his throat and adopted an irritating commentator-type voice. 'And here we have Magenta, Daniel's next-door neighbour and my on/off girlfriend.'

'Spud!' I snapped. 'I am *not* your on/off girlfriend!'

I made Magnus rewind that bit and Spud started again. 'So, Magenta, what would you like to say to Daniel so that he can remember you when he's hundreds of miles away?'

And that's when it hit me – Daniel was really going to be hundreds of miles away. And that's all I would be – a memory. All the times I'd gone over to see him and we'd sat on his bed, laughing and talking and doing artwork together; the times he'd come over to sort out my computer or help with my homework – they'd soon fade into the past. And all the silly, funny things we'd done together; the time last year when he got some of my glitter up his nose and sneezed all over me, the day I got bubble-gum in my hair in Year 7 and he had to cut it out really carefully, or when he taught me to skateboard – all resigned to history! My mind was filled with wonderful flashbacks of when we went out together – the kisses, the cuddles, the giggles. I'd been so happy when we were together, probably the happiest I'd ever been in my entire fourteen years (well, thirteen and eleven-twelfths), and now it was never going to be that way again. Daniel was just going to be another phase of my life,

like ballet lessons or primary school. It would be –
Oh, that was when Daniel lived next door. I couldn't bear
it.

Suddenly I found myself staring into the lens
of the video camera and my mind had gone into
meltdown. What could I say in a couple of sentences
that could possibly sum up everything I felt for him?

'Madge? You OK?' Arlette was shaking my arm as
though she was trying to wake me up.

'I can't do this,' I said. And then, the worst thing
ever happened – the big balloon in my chest burst
and I started to cry. On camera! I was blubbing and
snotting all over – how humiliating was that? 'Turn
it off,' I said, putting my hand over the lens.

'Come on, Madge,' Arlette said. 'You, of all people,
should say something. After all, Daniel's like your
soul mate.'

And she was right! He *is* my soul mate. How had I
never seen it before? I'd been so stupid and now it
was too late.

Magnus put the camera on the grass. 'Are you all
right, Magenta? You don't have to do this if you don't
want, you know.'

And then Spud bent down to offer me his hanky.
Which was quite sweet, I thought. I was so pleased
that there were no hard feelings since I finished with

him. Until I saw the disgusting snot rag he'd handed me to dry my eyes on!

'Ewww! Spud – that's so gross.'

'Sorry, Magenta, but you know I get hay fever.'

I handed it back. 'I suppose it's the thought that counts.' Which was very generous of me, in the circumstances.

'Here.' Arlette handed me a tissue. 'You know what, Madge,' she said. 'I think you should tell him. Not on the camera but to his face.' Then she started to get all deep and meaningful. 'I know I usually leave all the agony aunt stuff to Seema . . .' Uh oh! I was getting the distinct whiff of a *but* coming up. '. . . but . . .' Told you! '. . . as she's not here, I'm going to go out on a limb . . .' Oh, I dread it when Arl goes out on a limb. 'Everyone knows I've had the hots for Daniel for ages, so you know how hard it is for me to say this, but I think you should tell him how you feel about him before it's too late. It would be the worst thing ever if he went away thinking you didn't care.'

And then it happened again. It was like my tear ducts were totally out of control. I was blubbing like a baby. 'It's already too late,' I sobbed. 'Scotland has different term times to us and he starts his new school in a couple of weeks.' I took a deep breath and dried my eyes on Arlette's tissue then stood up. 'But you're right – I should do this. Where's that camera?' I said in the most businesslike voice I could manage.

Magnus picked up the camcorder and zoomed in on my face (a bit too close, actually – I certainly didn't want Daniel remembering me by the red blotches round my eyes). I forced my lips into a smile. 'Hi, Daniel, it's me, Magenta. I just want to say, you're the best mate a girl could wish for and life won't be the same without you.' Then I put my hand up to signal that I'd finished and took Arlette's arm. 'Come on, let's go see how Seema's doing.' I just wanted to get away.

'What about the card?' Spud asked, wafting it in our faces.

'We'll sign it later,' I called as we walked away.

As we made our way across the field, there was a roar from the athletics track and I looked up to see Kara Kennedy crossing the finishing line. She gave a victory punch in the air and Chad Albright ran across and handed her her tracksuit. I watched him put his arm round her shoulders and I didn't feel the teensiest bit jealous. Phew! At least that confirmed that I was well and truly over him. But then I saw Daniel go across to Kara, give her a peck on the cheek and a congratulatory thumbs-up. I felt as though a nest of vipers had just hatched in my tummy and were eating away at me from the inside. Then the overflow in my eye area began again. Uh oh! I needed to get away from everyone.

'I'm just going to the loo,' I said to Arlette. 'I'll see you back in the tutor room.'

Only I didn't go to the loo. I sneaked round the back of the Science block and bunked off. I knew The Blob would throw a mental, but what could she do with only one more day left? And who cares anyway?

Daniel's leaving do was the worst party in the entire history of parties – on many levels:

1) There were all Mary's friends from the hospital as well as Daniel's friends from school and, believe me, parties are not usually known to successfully cross the generation gap.

2) Mary had packed up all the decent CDs, so the music was from a compilation cassette that she'd bought in about 1989 and one of Donald's folk-dancing tapes.

3) The atmosphere was about as welcoming as a funeral parlour – there were only overhead lights because Mary had packed all the table lamps, most of the furniture was stacked up ready to go and all the little knick-knacks that made the place so homely were packed away

in boxes that were piled up all over the place.

4) The food was courtesy of Chez Florence – and we all know that my gran can't even cook toast without the emergency services being put on red alert!

5) Spud had had an image transplant and had turned up with slicked back hair and shades so that he looked like some second-rate extra from *The Matrix* in a disgusting Hawaiian shirt.

And finally,

6) Poor Daniel was moping about with his chin practically trailing on the ground. Not that he was the only one – in fact, there wasn't a single person there who looked remotely happy – except Donald, who was doing his best to drum up enthusiasm for the Gay Gordons.

'So, do you fancy a dance, then, Magenta?' Spud lifted his shades and winked at me. 'I was just thinking, now Daniel's moving away maybe we could give it another go?'

I hadn't done country-dancing since Year 4 and I certainly was *not* in the mood for Spud's pathetic attempt at flirting. 'Exactly which part of "dumped" are you struggling to grasp, Spud?'

'But I thought . . .'

'Well, don't think! For one thing, it doesn't suit you

and for another, you don't have the right equipment!'

It was probably a bit harsh, but I was trying to keep myself from dissolving into a weeping wimp again. So I took that as my cue to leave the sitting room and headed for the kitchen to get a drink of Coke. Most of the adults seemed to have congregated there in order to avoid being press-ganged into Donald's impromptu barn dance.

'So, Mary, love,' I heard Gran saying as I approached the kitchen door. 'Have you got a new job yet? When will you start? Is there a hospital near where you're going to live or will you work for a doctors' surgery?'

Mary shook her head. 'Not yet, Florence, I'll probably wait till we're settled in before I start looking.'

'And what about the house?' Belinda asked. 'I can't believe they pulled out at such short notice.'

Mary shrugged. 'These things happen. Anyway, I've put it back on the market. Donald's got a holiday home on the banks of the loch, so we'll live there till I get a buyer for this. We can't afford to buy the fish farm till this is sold though.'

Great! So I was going to be living next door to an empty house after Monday. How spooky was that going to be? Although I suppose it was marginally preferable to the family from hell with three screaming brats who had been going to move in.

I'd decided to pass on the Coke and go and find someone who was marginally nearer to my own age and who wasn't dressed like a sleazy holiday rep, eager to whisk me off in a dozy-doe, when I heard Dad's voice. 'And how's Daniel coping?'

'Amazingly well, actually,' Mary replied.

Huh! So much for Arl's first attempt at agony aunt! It's a good job I didn't follow her advice and go blurting out that I'd miss him. What a prat I'd've looked. I felt a lump of lead descend into my feet. I was just about to make my excuses and go home when I heard Seema. She was leaning over the banister and beckoning me upstairs.

'Madge – come on! We're going to give Daniel his leaving present.'

I went upstairs but Daniel's room was so full there were people spilling out on to the landing. Honestly, I never knew he had so many friends. There were even people from Year 10 and that Samantha girl from the sixth form had turned up too. I could see Magnus handing over the enormous card everyone had signed. Well, everyone except me – oops! I couldn't see Daniel though. I think he must've been sitting on the bed or something. I caught sight of

Spud (correction, I caught sight of half a ton of hair wax in sunglasses) standing in front of Daniel's open French windows clutching a package. And then an awful thought occurred to me. Ohmigod! I just hoped Magnus had had the common sense to edit out the part on the video when I'd started crying.

There were too many people to squeeze through, so I decided to quickly run downstairs, back to our house, and then go through my bedroom and round by the balcony. That way I'd be able to have a word with Spud before he gave the tape to Daniel. My plan was to take it down to Dad's VCR and have a sneaky look. If necessary, I decided I might even have to swap it with one of Dad's home videos until I could get hold of Dad's camcorder and rerecord my bit.

It was starting to get dark but, luckily, Belinda had lent Mary some fairy lights to trail along the balcony to try and make the place look a little bit more festive. In any other circumstances they'd have looked really sweet and magical draped along the wisteria that grows along Daniel's side of the balcony.

Daniel was still reading messages off the card when I sneaked up behind Spud, tapped him on the shoulder and beckoned for him to come out on to the balcony.

'Yo!' He spun round like he was expecting a Wild West gunman to be pointing a six-shooter at him.

'Sssh! For goodness sake, Spud, don't be so dramatic,' I whispered. I can't stand people who make a drama festival out of nothing. 'Can I borrow the video for a couple of minutes?' I stretched up and whispered in his ear, so that none of the others could hear.

'No way!' he said, backing away from me and clutching it to his chest.

'I'll bring it straight back,' I promised.

'No!'

'Spud!' It was becoming imperative to get the tape from Spud. The last thing I wanted was for Daniel's abiding memory of me to be where I was blubbing everywhere. 'Just give me the tape.'

I reached out and tried to grab it but Spud was too quick for me.

'Leave it out, Magenta!' he said, holding the video above his head.

I lunged at him but he leaned back, out of my reach. He had his back against the wrought iron balustrade and I was trying desperately to grab the video from him. 'Gimme!' I was starting to panic.

'Magenta?' Uh-oh! It was Daniel. He'd finished reading the card and had come out to see what the commotion was. 'What's going on? I haven't seen you all evening.'

'Er, hi!' I spun round to face him. But, as I turned, my elbow accidentally caught Spud on the chin.

'Ow!' Spud yelled, followed by an ominous, 'Oh, oh, oh, oh – aaaaaaagh!' as he lost his balance and toppled backwards – right over the edge of Daniel's balcony!

Daniel lurched forwards and grabbed Spud's foot – just in time. Wow! He was so quick, he was amazing. 'Help me!' he called, as Spud dangled upside down by one leg with his arms flailing about like a windmill.

Suddenly there were about a million people on the balcony all trying to pull Spud back up. In fact, the whole structure was beginning to feel distinctly wobbly. 'Everyone back inside!' Daniel shouted. 'No more than three people on here at a time. Magnus, you grab his other foot. Magenta, we'll hold him here while you go back and get one of the adults to lower him down.'

Wow – how amazing is Daniel? I just stood there on the balcony in the fairy lights and looked at him for a second – he was just so calm and so wonderful – the way he knew exactly what to do in a crisis.

'Now, Magenta!' he snapped – but not in a nasty way. In fact he sounded really manly and authoritative.

'Just going!'

I ran back down through our house and was just going to go back into Daniel's front door, when there was an ominous cracking sound; I couldn't make out if it was the balcony, the wisteria or Spud's legs. Then a length of guttering crashed to the ground right in front of me and the string of fairy lights fell down and draped themselves round Spud's neck.

Spud started yelling, 'I'm slipping, I'm slipping!'

'Quick!' Daniel called down to me. 'We're going to try and swing him into the hedge. Magenta, when we let go, you try to guide him over to the right.'

Hmmm! 'My right, or Spud's right?' I shouted up.

'Never mind whose right – just push him towards the hedge after three.' Did I say, Daniel sounded manly? Well, forget it, he was beginning to sound plain bossy. 'OK – one ...' An upside-down Spud swung to the left.

'It's OK,' I shouted up, 'I've just realised, they're both the same.'

'What?' Daniel called.

'My right and Spud's right – they're the same.'

'Brilliant!' Ooooo! Sarcastic, or what? I might just

have to re-evaluate my opinion of him. '. . . two . . .'

Again Spud moved towards me.

I braced myself. 'I'm ready!'

'I'm not!' screamed Spud.

'. . . three!' yelled Daniel.

We had lift-off! As Daniel and Magnus released their grip on Spud's feet, I pushed him in the ribs and watched as he was propelled into the privet hedge that ran along the side of Daniel's path. Yes! Success! The eagle had landed safely. Phew! How brilliant was that!

Spud sat up. He had bits of privet stuck to his hair wax, his shades were at an angle of forty-five degrees over one ear and he had flashing fairy lights dangling round his neck. 'Wow!' he said. 'That was amazing. I don't suppose you'd reconsider going out with me, would you?'

Grrr! Can you believe him? 'How many times do I have to tell you, I do not want to go out with you.'

'Oh, go on. We make a great team.'

'Spud!' My relief that he'd landed safely was fast turning into exasperation. 'I don't love you. I love Daniel. OK?'

'What did you just say?' Oooops! It was Daniel. He'd come downstairs and was standing right behind me.

'Erm . . . I was just saying that I didn't want to go out with Spud.'

'I meant after that.' He was looking at me in this really weird way.

Oh boy! How was I going to get out of this one? But I needn't have worried. I didn't have to get out of it. Daniel looked right into my eyes till I thought my whole stomach had turned to blancmange.

'I love you too, Magenta.'

Then he leaned forwards and kissed me. Just like that, with everyone looking at us and Spud's fairy lights twinkling from the hedge.

It was sooooo romantic!

P.S.

Didn't I tell you I always look on the positive side? I knew everything would turn out for the best.

After Daniel had given me the dreamiest, most knee-wobbling kiss ever, we went into the house to find Mary. (Well, we helped Spud out of the hedge first of course, although, to be honest, I was pretty tempted to leave him there for a while, to cool off.)

Anyway, Daniel was holding my hand and he dragged me into the kitchen where Mary was talking to the other adults.

'Mum, I know this probably messes everything up and I know it's really short notice and I know I've got my place in school organised and everything but . . .' You could've heard a hair clip drop it was so quiet – except for some ancient Barry Manilow song from the other room. '. . . I'm not going to go to Scotland.'

Everyone gasped, like the ending of a murder mystery when they suddenly announce who the killer is.

'But why?' If you've ever seen a balloon that's gone

down and is all shrunken and caved in, well that's what Mary looked like. 'I thought you were OK with the whole thing.'

'I was . . . well . . . I wasn't really.' And then he gave me this really gooey smile till my tummy did back flips. 'I was only going away 'cos I thought Magenta didn't want to go out with me any more.'

'But I do!' I said. Well, I thought I ought to say something to break the tension.

Mary looked like she was going to burst into tears. Someone pulled a stool from the top of the pile of furniture in the corner and she slumped down on it. 'I think we need to talk about this, Daniel, before you make any hasty decisions.'

'This isn't a hasty decision.' Daniel kept smiling at me and squeezing my hand. Oooo, it was so lovely to be going out with him again. 'I'm sorry, Mum, but this is what I want. I'll go and see The Crusher tomorrow. I'm sure he'll let me have my place back at school and I can go to live at Dad's with Joe.'

And that's when Donald, Daniel's stepdad, came up trumps! 'Och, laddie, there's no need to go putting yourself through that. The solution's simple.'

And it was! Donald pointed out that Mary's house hadn't been sold and it wasn't as though they'd got anywhere to go in Scotland yet, so he was willing to wait for his fish farm till Daniel had finished his education. How amazing is that? They're all going to stay here and carry on living next door! And, even better, Joe said he'd probably spend half his time with his dad from now on! Oh yes! Result!

The other good thing that happened is that we found the videotape in the middle of the hedge and Daniel says he thinks it's really cute the way I was crying and stuff. He's so sweet. Do I have the most amazing boyfriend in the world, or what?

So, here we all are, in the woods next to the reservoir. The whole place is lit up with tea lights hanging from the trees in little jars and the sun's just going down so there's the most magical pink light everywhere. It is soooo romantic. I want my wedding to be just like this.

I know at one time I was a teensy little bit anxious about the dresses Belinda had designed but, to be honest, I never really doubted her – she's so talented. I know I wanted to wear the pink sari fabric one but, honestly, the one Belinda made me is soooo sophisticated. It's in this gorgeous pale green, with a sort of goldy-coloured batik pattern round the hem, and it's got long sleeves that flare out. Daniel says I look like a medieval maiden. Oooooo, he's so lovely.

And round the edge of the sleeves and the neck, Mrs Hemmings has done some embroidery in gold to match the batik. Belinda said, strictly speaking it wasn't organic or biodegradable, but she knew I'd like it – she's so thoughtful.

And you should see what she's wearing. Oh my God! She looks so beautiful. She's like a proper fairytale bride. She's got her hair loose and it comes halfway down her back and she's wearing a dress that's the same style as mine but it's in unbleached cotton with a long train. And guess what? I get to carry the train all on my own because my cousins from hell have contracted chickenpox and can't come! How lucky is that?

There was the teensiest bit of trauma earlier because Gran wanted to bring the bride on the back of her motorbike but Belinda said it wasn't environmentally friendly. Anyway, in the end they compromised and Gran pedalled one of those rickshaw tricycles with Belinda and me in the back. Which, I have to admit, was a bit scary every time we went round a corner, but at least it meant that Gran could wear her leathers. And it only took a few minutes to get our hair sorted out again and away from the hurricane look.

It's not like any other wedding I'd ever been

to because Belinda and I are walking through this avenue of trees, and people are blowing bubbles for us to walk through till we get to the clearing where Dad's waiting. Even Sirius is sitting there, chewing his vegetable protein bone.

There aren't any pews or seats, everyone's just standing around watching while Dad and Belinda say their vows to each other. Which is brilliant because it means that Daniel and I can stand next to each other the whole time and hold hands. Oooo, this is so dreamy, it's not true!

And now the minister has asked Dad and Belinda to exchange rings. Wow! Daniel has only lifted up my hand as well – and now he's gazing into my eyes and pushing this fabulous silver ring on to my thumb. I think my insides are melting I'm so happy.

He's smiling at me. 'This is an early birthday present, to replace the one you lost at bowling.' Oooo, I've gone all tingly. But, uh-oh – now he's got his serious look on – not usually a good sign. 'You're the only girl I've ever loved, you know, Magenta.' Phwoar! He can get as serious as he likes if he's going to say things like that.

And guess what? The ring's only engraved with *Daniel + Magenta 4 ever*.

Oooooo, I do love happy endings!

A note from the author

Yet again, I have my brother Martin to thank for the inspiration for some of Magenta's antics. We went on a school trip to Paris when I was ten and he was nine. One day we went to a very exclusive department store on the Île de la Cité, an island in the middle of the river Seine … and no prizes for guessing what happened. One minute Martin was twiddling a piece of string, the next there was mayhem as an enormous rubber dinghy unfurled in the middle of the shop! And, yes, he did run the wrong way down the up escalator with all the shop staff running after him, shouting in French! They always say that fact is stranger than fiction.

MAGENTA ORANGE

Echo Freer

Magenta Orange has the world at her feet. If she could just stop tripping over them.

Bright, sassy and massively accident prone, Magenta's seen as a jinx by her mates – and a disaster zone by the boy of her dreams. Blind to the longing looks of her best friend, Daniel, and the sweet nothings of school freak, Spud, she's set her sights on year 11 hottie, Adam Jordan – and she'll risk everything, even total humiliation, in her relentless pursuit of a date . . .

'A wicked, witty read – 5/5!' *Mizz* magazine

MAGENTA IN THE PINK

Echo Freer

Magenta Orange is back – and this time she's centre stage . . .

Magenta is desperate to star in the school production of Grease – she's always fancied being a Pink Lady – but chaos at the casting means she ends up stuck firmly behind the scenes. And it's not long before she's getting into trouble again – developing a crush on the leading man, accidentally sabotaging the scenery and trashing ex boyfriend Daniel's skateboard in a vain attempt to impress hunky bad boy Ryan. Now it's not just the set crashing around her ears, but all her dreams of super-stardom and snogging too . . .

BLAGGERS

Echo Freer

Mercedes Bent is trying to go straight – if only her family weren't so crooked . . .

Mercedes has carved herself a nice little niche at the Daphne Pincher Academy for Young Ladies, running a sweepstake and taking bets on anything that moves. The only fly in the ointment is her arch-rival, gangster's daughter Harley 'halitosis' Spinks. How come *she's* got the great work placement and Mercedes has ended up in a boring bank?

But things start to look up when Mercedes wangles a date with the bank's hottest young trainee, Zak – until she finds out that it's not just the Spinks gang who are into dodgy dealing; her own brothers are as crooked as a pair of corkscrews too! It's a safe bet that Mercedes will have to keep her family's illegal activities under wraps – if she's to have even an outside chance with the boy of her dreams . . .